SPUN GOLD

CHRISTIS CHRISTIE

Midnight Tide
PUBLISHING

For my Grammie,
who believed in my writing so much, she carried one of my high
school short stories around in her purse so that she could make
everyone she met read it.

Chapter One

I was born a blight upon the beauty and grace that is the elven world; a deformed creature that had no rights or place among their society. While most babes are born to them a pearl of perfection, I held the resemblance of a newly hatched bird with colourless skin not flushed with life, and the pinched features of a hobgoblin—a nose too long, ears too pointed, and dark, bottomless eyes that spoke of the depths of the world's despair rather than the light of possibility and life.

My parents cast me out into the cold winter harshness in hopes that the frozen fingers of Frau Holle would claim me. Instead of being pulled down into the finality of the afterlife as was intended, two trolls found my wailing form.

Those of the elven nature are known for carrying magic in their blood, and to feast upon them, for many other creatures, is not only a delight, but a way of absorbing some of that magical essence into themselves. Too frail and feeble to make for good eating, though, I was bundled in a scrap piece of cloth and taken back to their dwelling in the dank depths of the earth.

There, in the subtle dimness of Grolge and Klimn's cave, I was fed and nurtured alongside other stolen cattle. The goats accepted me well enough, letting the straw of their pen act as my cradle, and offering milk meant for their own young to fill my hungry maw. I filled out quickly on that sweet offering, becoming the fatty morsel worthy of roasting on the open fire and grinding between large troll teeth as had been intended. But Grolge and Klimn were stupid beings who quarrelled over the faintest slight and couldn't decide who should get the babe that would be but a snack to creatures of their size.

It started as a discussion that soon escalated into an outright battle that nearly destroyed the cave and left me inches from being crushed beneath Klimn's foot. In the end, it was decided that I would be allowed to grow more, and until I had reached a size that was acceptable for sharing, they would make use of me and my magic. I suppose in a lot of ways, my stunted form that was shunned by my elven parents actually saved my life. By the time I was of any decent size, barely above the head of our tallest ram, my magic had proven too useful to dispose of, even considering the quick rush of pleasure feasting on it would provide them.

With the threat of ending up spitted and roasted overshadowing my days, I turned into a clever survivor who continued to find new means of proving my living worth. Mortals, it turned out, are nearly as stupid as the cave trolls who kept me, and even as a small child, I found it easy to distract them so that larger cattle could be stolen to feed the abyss inside my large counterparts. Shepherds and cowherds were perhaps the easiest to manipulate, their boredom leaving them open for trickery. I laid traps, caused confusing noises and other disturbances that they couldn't help but leave their posts to check on.

After that, it took nothing to spell the animals into following me into the woods and back to the cave. With me around, the trolls barely had to lift a finger anymore, each meal walking compliantly into their awaiting arms. Of course, even simple-minded creatures end up longing for more than their means, and eventually Grolge and Klimn came to the conclusion that they were not aiming high enough with my trickery. No, there was a far tastier feast to be had than Farmer Bram's prized milk cows.

I was perhaps ten years of age, still stunted in height and haggard in appearance, when the spark of new hunger arose in them.

"Oi, Rumpelstiltskin! Stop rattlin' those posts, you worthless pophart and come here," Grolge bellowed that morning, just seconds before the thighbone of a calf came hurtling at my unsuspecting head.

Pain lanced through my skull that had borne many such attacks over the years, and for the briefest of moments, I allowed my eyes to close upon the cave surrounding me and just breathed. But moving at my own leisure had never been the way of life, so soon I was on my feet and leaving behind the goat pen I was attempting to mend. After a battle the previous night over Klimn picking his teeth too loudly with a rib bone, the pen had been demolished, and no one but I was going to fix it.

I didn't say anything, only trudged over to the large lump of leather and scaly flesh that made up Grolge.

"Me and Klimn, we's been thinkin', we have. We're tired of cows." In his large paw there was the head of a calf he'd cracked open and was in the process of slurping at the brains while he spoke. It was enough to turn one's stomach if one wasn't used to it.

"No more cows," Klimn felt it necessary to chime in.

I felt a dawning suspicion beginning to sprout within my young mind, one I didn't want to actually contemplate, and thus did not give voice to.

"So, what do you wish instead?"

In the rare times that I was left to my own devices, I had taken to watching the humans. My favourite pastime was becoming one with the shadows so that I could spy on them for hours. Other than an initial chill of foreboding, the mortals always remained blissfully unaware of my eyes in the dark. It was how I learned their ways, their behaviours, and their speech. How I saw both the best and the worst of them, and came to understand that at their most primitive, they weren't that different from the trolls, and in their more evolved form, they hungered for power—or the semblance of it.

I knew how to draw them in—how to play them.

"Man."

"Or woman," Klimn grunted.

"Or woman. But no cows, and if no human..." Grolge leaned towards me, the stench of his putrid breath strong in my nose. "Then you."

The blunt tip of his large finger tapped me in the chest and sent me reeling backwards on my bottom in the dirt. A war raged in my head, a battle between my keen wits and the desire to roll my eyes in annoyance. Ever the same threat, without any evidence it would actually take place. Though, one could never put it past their stupidity to eat their own meal ticket.

"Fine. Humans." As elegantly as possible, I picked myself up off the floor and dusted the dirt from my slacks. They were the only pair I owned, and only because I had tricked a stupid peasant boy into giving them to me by convincing him that the stolen goose I held in my clutches laid golden eggs.

The trade had been well worth it, in my mind.

With both trolls having made up their minds on the same thing, I had little choice but to leave in that moment and set out towards the village. One can think me heartless if they want, but I felt little sorrow for the human I was bound to lead to their death. I had not been brought up to feel any softness for them, and what I had seen of their kind had not helped any to sprout.

My legs were not of any substantial length, but still I made quick timing through the woods that concealed our cave and up into the open plains of the green fields that surrounded the local village. Here, flock upon flock of sheep grazed, their full coats as yet unshaven, resembling that of fluffy, rounded clouds, meandering lazily over the hills.

I didn't have to think of who it was I would bring back—all my time human-watching had left a very clear first victim in my mind. One who, as I saw it, almost deserved the fate about to end him. Blond-headed Karl was a mean-spirited boy who often taunted the other shepherds, and his crook, which was meant to aid him in traversing the hills, was more often than not used to viciously jab or beat the sheep in his flock out of his own way. Not but two days before, I had witnessed him throw another herder to the ground, land a well-placed kick to his side, and then make off with his lunch. So, I felt absolutely no remorse as I slipped up behind him on the hill.

"That is a tasty morsel you are eating there... If you share it with me, I will tell you where I just saw Greta Schulz bathing in nothing but her petticoat not but five minutes ago."

The boy jumped in his seat, startled into a gasp by the sudden sound of my voice whispering behind his back. The sight of me, as he leaped quickly from his perch on the boulder, was the standard one gifted to me by the general populace in the rare occasions when I allowed myself to be seen. His features scrunched in disgust, similar to when someone inhaled a sour scent.

"What are you, creature, and why should I believe anything that you say?"

My less-than-appealing appearance had placed some

hesitation within him, but I was still able to read the desire for what I had offered in the depths of his eyes. His lusty, needy character was selfish enough to look past a suspicious nature and the potential of harm to himself, for the thrilling thought of a clandestine peeping moment in the woods. He was also just stupid enough to believe that something as puny as myself would be unable to do any real injury to him in the end.

"What I am does not matter for the purpose of our agreement. However, what I can do for you does. Greta won't be in the water for long—now is your time to decide; give up the food and find the location or sit back down and never know. *Tick tock*, the clock is ticking. Don't spend too much time thinking it over or you'll miss your chance entirely."

What I had long ago discovered about humans was that the less time you gave them to think, and the more panicked you caused them to become, the more likely they were to make very terrible decisions without weighing the cost.

Karl stuttered and stammered, shifting on his feet before me, and then thrust the bratwurst, nestled in a lush bread roll and buried beneath juicy sauerkraut, into my awaiting hands. Staring down at my prized achievement, it was necessary to fight the desire to lick my lips. Too often, my food portions were made up of whatever puny scraps were left over from the ravenous trolls, bits and pieces of half chewed veal spat from their mouth during an angry comment to the other. But this...this was a prize indeed.

"Well?" Karl grunted. "I've given you what you demanded. Are you going to take me or not?"

If truth would be told, I had forgotten for the time being that he was there or that I had other things I was meant to be doing, and it irritated me to have my attention pulled away from the delight in my hands. But my life was not my own and if I came back empty-handed, there was always the possibility that I could become the next meal Klimn and Grolge fed upon.

"Right, of course. Follow me, young master," I declared to him and then made a formal bow. That brought his head up straighter and chased farther away any doubts resting at the back of his mind.

It then took no time for me to lead the stupid, vile boy into the woods, assuring him that Greta was just around the next cluster of trees or beyond the riverbank. When at last we came to the opening of the cave, confusion dawned in his eyes, before being replaced with dawning suspicion. But it was too late at this point, and my true masters, having scented human on the winds, made their way out of the cave depths and were upon him shortly. I turned away from the howls and cries, leaving Klimn and Grolge to their feeding, and found a pleasant spot to sit and enjoy the meal I had managed to acquire for myself.

That wasn't the last time that I was sent out into the local village to pillage a human meal for the creatures raising me, and knowing that there would be no stopping them once the taste of blood was upon their tongues, my only hope was to convince them to leave some time between each human life taken. The last thing that any of us needed was to raise enough suspicion that the village came searching the woods, pitchforks in hand.

CHAPTER TWO

I became incredibly skilled in convincing all different walks of life to follow me deep into the woods, learning to read the unspoken desires on the faces of each new victim, seeing the lines of imperfection that ran just below the skin like a well-drawn map leading me directly to their greatest weakness. It should have bothered me the older I became, but instead I took pleasure in each new deception, and when that became too easy, I grew bored with it and I turned it into a game. Giving them ways to win their freedom, but knowing that the odds I had given them were stacked too high—and yet not entirely impossible.

As the years passed, I maintained my connection to the human world, venturing to the villages on my own time so that I could continue watching from my shadows. I longed to learn all that I could about the mortals, as it was a world outside my own. Seeing as how there seemed to be no real place for me in the world of magic, perhaps I could find a place amongst them.

In the end, I learned a valuable lesson in the small village of Freudenshafen, where I first saw Lina Schneider seated on a grassy knoll, braiding alpine poppies into flower crowns to place on the heads of her younger sisters. Her copper hair reflected the light of living flames in the bright sunlight of the summer day, and her pale freckled cheeks glowed with an inner warmth that spoke of happiness and laughter.

That particular field was her favourite place to spend her afternoons, and once she had finished with her household chores, Lina would slip away from her parents' home with either her siblings in tow, or on her own. There, with her skirts settled about her folded legs, she would work on sewing, paint little portraits of wildflowers with her simple set of paints, or simply bask in the warm sunlight.

For days on end, I crept into the same small cluster of trees on the edge of her field, just so that I could watch her, my breath bated and my heart pitter-pattering rapidly in my chest. Whereas with anyone else, I felt no hesitation in making my presence known, with her, I warred against doubt and fear of the unknown.

It was Lina, in the end, who made contact first. On a quiet summer day, the sun already well past the noon-day high, she looked directly into my little hiding place, blue eyes piercing through the underbrush, and seemed to peer directly at me.

"Are you ever going to come out and introduce yourself?"

Very little in life managed to surprise me by this point. But that day, nestled snugly between two small bushes with a bed of fallen leaves beneath my body, I thought myself completely hidden from view. Yet Lina had peered through my covering and seen me anyway—perhaps seen me the whole time. A little part of myself belonged to her that day, so startled was I to be found out by anyone, least of all my fiery-headed girl.

There was hesitation in my response—what would be her reaction to the sight of me in clear daylight, the sunshine highlighting my unsightly appearance in all its gory details, the dark, bottomless eyes set deep within my face, a harsh sloping nose that pointed too sharply, and long, elfin ears that seemed too over-pronounced, rather than the delicate pieces of art they were meant to be? The teeth in my small mouth were pointed, and my hair, which was so light blond it was nearly white, would have been lovely, if not for the greyish pallor of my flesh. I was garish in comparison to her fresh youthfulness, and yet I slowly crept from the under-brush to crouch in a manner that would make it easy to dart off, should the situation become too unpleasant for me.

Shock did register in her eyes as she beheld me for the first time. Up until this point, I had been nothing but a set of watchful eyes in the leaves, not the horrid little creature now kneeling before her. While there was a touch of revulsion, this seemed to fade as she gazed at me, a look of curiosity and interest soon replacing it.

"Come here," she requested of me, going so far as to pat a spot of grass beside her.

Carefully, I stood to my full height, that could be no more than four feet—I'd never really thought to test this out for specifics—and then slowly made my way over to her. My heart that was typically so calm and unfazed beat rapidly against the ribcage surrounding it.

I didn't go quite as near as she had offered, but stopped once there were roughly five steps left between us, and then sat opposite her so that we were able to look into each other's eyes. Hers were as crystal-clear as a fresh brook, and a lovely shade of blue that would make the heavens above weep in jealousy. Mine, in contrast, were reminiscent of the dark, shadowy green of the forest in the places where the sunlight is but a light filtering through the leaves and needles.

"Who are you?" Not *what* are you.

As of that point, I had said nothing—not a sound or gasp, barely an indrawn breath—but something about the way she posed her question loosened my hesitant tongue.

"I haven't a name, but they call me Rumpelstiltskin," I admitted, without elaborating on 'they.'

Those clear eyes were watching me again, flitting over my face in an intelligent manner, before lowering to take in my frame, mindful of my hands with their sharp little claws, and then back up to my face.

"Rumpelstiltskin? Like some form of pophart?" she questioned me, and caused a pinched look of discomfort to form upon my features. "Are you a goblin, then?"

"Yes, like a pophart. And no, not like a goblin, at least I do not think so." There was no real explanation for what I was. Were goblins naught but castaway elves who failed to meet the standards of a perfectionist society?

"That is a cruel name." Her words—soft and honest, filled with concern for my being—were a foreign notion.

Having never known care nor worry for myself to come from another being, I simply stared at her. Who was this divine angel gazing back at me with such tenderness and lack of fear? She claimed a little more of me then.

"It is but a name, and we are made up of more."

"Would you care for some *maultaschen*?" From inside a pocket in her apron, she pulled a cloth bundle. Setting the bundle between us, her slender fingers swiftly unknotted it to reveal small little pastry dumplings filled with something that smelled delicious.

With good, wholesome food before me, I did not hesitate to take what was offered, and soon the flavour of savoury pork was coating my tongue and I felt a great new fondness for this thing called *maultaschen*.

"Why have you been watching me? It's not polite to creep upon someone from the woods. Is that how you always behave?" She was attempting, in her best mature, young woman voice, to scold me into feeling guilty for my actions, and while I had a growing appreciation inside me for this red-haired young angel, it would take much more than a gentle voice turned firm to make me rethink my ways.

"It's better to go about my day in the shadows than be chased away by fearful lads or angry shepherds thinking I am out for their sheep."

"Well, no more hiding with me. It is far easier to trust a being you can see before you, than one lurking in the bushes."

From that point on, a strange little friendship sprouted between us, and I would flee the darkness of the troll cave to spend as much time as I was allotted in the presence of the lovely Lina. She fed me whatever delicious treat she pilfered from her mother's kitchen, introduced me as the spirit of the woods to her younger siblings, and all in all, taught me what it was like to look forward to each new day.

For the first time in my life, I had a friend, and the notion of it sparked a new sort of light into my existence—one that made the cave I dwelt in a little brighter, and the thought of dealing with the trolls just a little easier to bear. Grolge had questioned me on different occasions about where I disappeared most days, but humans weren't the only ones I was skilled in fooling and evading. Always, I managed to have him so twisted up in his thoughts by the time that we were done, that he would forget what he had asked me to begin with, and Klimn only aided me in my endeavours by intervening with equally confusing and incoherent asides.

But the ideal life cannot last, and either I became too sure of myself and my convincing ways, or Grolge was smarter than I took him for.

It was a sunny day—the sky blue and cloudless—when everything began to go downhill. After bringing the trolls a buck from the woods, I left them to their feasting and slipped into the trees, following the small path that had begun to wear from my constant travelling, and took myself off to the grassy knoll where my Lina was bound to be. She hadn't arrived yet, and so I sat in the bushes waiting, wishing to see the moment she appeared in the clearing, unaware that she was being watched, lovely and free.

As her copper head came suddenly into my line of vision, I felt the breath steal from my chest and the quickening pace of my heart and, not for the first time I wondered if perhaps this was what it felt like to care...to love. Was this the attachment I had heard so many of the mortals talking about—the thing that pushed them into foolish behaviour that embarrassed them all for the sake of wooing the item of their affection? I had thought it impossible—that I was beyond such considerations—but Lina had awoken something strange inside me.

Though I hadn't heard the crunch of leaves behind me, I was not so ignorant to my surroundings that I failed to feel the lifting of the hair at the back of my neck, as a chill of foreboding crept over me, and the large shadow chased away the sun, along with my happiness. The stench of putrid flesh and dank earth greeted me and announced the presence of the troll to my back.

"She's a pretty lil' creature, int'she?"

Grolge, apparently not as preoccupied with venison as I had thought him to be, had managed to follow the path I'd left through the forest, and found my small personal haven.

"She's just a girl," I tried to tell him, keeping my tone indifferent while a light sweat broke out along my hairline.

"Justa girl," he repeated. "I wan'er. She looks much tastier than that deer ya brought me."

In that very moment, I had entered into the nightmare of my existence—nighttime terrors made real. At my sides, my hands balled into fists and began to glow with a faint light as my magic awoke within me. However, as badly as I wanted to strike out at him, I dared not—my magic was far too untested against something of his size, and should I fail, it would mean my own death—an outcome I had been fighting against all my life.

"No."

"What?"

It had come out more firmly than I had intended, but there it was.

"No. Not her. I will bring you two others instead."

He was hesitating, and eyeing Lina with a look that did not bode well for either of us. My own appreciation for her was clearly mirrored in him, but in the form of hunger.

"Two others, and you may siphon some of my magic." There would only be one way. To open my wrist and allow him to drink, hoping that he didn't take so much that he would kill me—or become addicted to the sensation of magic coursing through him and force this upon me until he had drunk me ragged and empty.

A new hunger filled his eyes as he peered down at me, his large maw gaping in a ravenous, gluttonous fashion, and I knew then that I had him. That for today, Lina Schneider was safe from the cave trolls hidden deep in the forest.

"Magic, now," he rumbled at me, and having been left no other choice, I turned from the field with only one last longing look and disappeared into the trees with Grolge to follow him back.

Hours later, when I was recovered enough from the blood loss, I went off to find him the two that I had promised. Mind hazy and cluttered with thoughts, I took the first two that I could find. A set of brothers that I typically overlooked due to their kind natures, but that day had already seen me sacrifice what I could for another—I had nothing else to give.

I allowed several weeks to elapse without returning to that special clearing and allowing myself to see Lina. Weeks in which I feared I would lead Grolge back there, and this time Klimn would join us, leaving me unable to stop the two of them from massacring everyone present. Weeks in which I allowed Grolge to sup from my veins multiple times, using me as his living supply of magic, during which I saw a whole new sort of hell opening up before me.

Eventually, I needed the light and happiness that my dear Lina offered me. So, I fled the cave and raced through the forest to our field.

She was already there upon her favourite knoll, a thick quilt spread out beneath her as she basked in the sunshine, practicing an even stitch that would make her tailor father proud. With my eyes latched on the welcome sight of her, I didn't hesitate and ran straight into the clearing, moving as quickly as the speed of my short legs would take me, and a growing smile spreading over my face—too quickly—too distracted to notice the three boys messing about in the creek just below, waded in up to their calves with their slacks rolled up to their knees.

"Lina! Watch out!"

The shout of one of them came before I had reached her, only halfway across the field. Our eyes met across the grassy expanse, alpine poppies and long grass swaying in the soft breeze between us, and then there was naught to do but cast our eyes down the hill to where the three young males were stampeding towards me, threateningly raised sticks in hand.

Startled at this sudden change in circumstances, I came to a halt so quickly that I stumbled, bare toes catching on turf and lurching me forward so that I tumbled and rolled, the breath knocked out of me. I had barely gathered my senses to me, and the boys had beset me, several whacks of the sticks landing upon my head or shoulders before Lina's shout pierced the air, ceasing all activity for the moment.

"No! Stop, please don't do that!"

With the trickle of blood at my temple, I climbed unsteadily to my feet, trying to put as much distance between myself and my attackers as I was able to. They wore surprised expressions upon their faces, having not expected to be asked to halt their act of supreme heroism.

"Lina, this little horrid goblin was coming after you!"

"He was going to attack you, Lina, likely going for blood."

"Or something more vile—they steal children and young women, you know."

She was upon her feet by this point and coming towards us all, looking like a queen in all her grace, red hair braided in a thick crown around her head.

"He's not a horrid goblin. Rumpelstiltskin is just a silly little creature who comes to visit with me here in the glen. He's harmless."

Silly little creature.

The boys gazed at her with looks of shock at this admission, but I had forgotten the trio of would-be heroes as a chill had spread through my form, joining the aches and pains already throbbing there. I was but a silly little creature to her, nothing but a spot of amusement in her day—nothing more than a pitiful animal to shed a little care upon when it presented itself. And yet, she had been my world.

I hardly registered the first jab of the stick in my side. The tallest boy was jeering at me in a sinister way as he spoke.

"You spend time with this thing, Lina? Look at it, it looks like it's half dead and has dragged itself through someone else's grave." His words were followed by another jab of the stick, and this time I reacted by stepping back a little. I should have responded or retaliated, but the world had crumbled at my feet.

"Stop poking him, Gerhard," Lina interjected.

"Did she say Rumpelstiltskin?" The plump boy, who gazed at Gerhard waiting for cues on how to react, soon added into the mix.

"Yes, Rumpelstilt. Rumpel. Rumpel. Rumpelstiltskin!" The

shortest boy of the bunch also seemed to be the angriest, and with each announcement of my so-called name, jabbed at me in a vicious sort of manner that had me lurching back in an attempt to be free of it.

Scrapes and scratches began to form on my tender flesh, the present state of my malnourishment not able to withstand the rough treatment.

"Wilhelm, stop that, you're going to hurt him!"

"Awww, Wilhelm, please don't hurt him." Gerhard sneered in a mocking tone. His eyes had filled with a jealous light at the way Lina defended me.

He, too, jabbed at me, but by that point I was becoming fed up with the poking and prodding of sharp sticks into my chest and sides and grabbed at it. Our eyes met across the stick, and we came to understand each other quite clearly. I hissed and he sneered more.

"I say kill it."

"Or at least chase it off," the well-fed one said, apparently with less of a killing streak than his comrades.

"Yes, Rumpelstiltskin, go off and rattle your little posts elsewhere, you haggard little goblin!"

A chorus of Rumpelstiltskins rang out around me, the clack of their sticks hitting against each other echoing in the open field. The trio then surrounded me, jabbing and hitting with their sticks in what had quickly become a whirlwind of noise and pain. There is only so much even a small creature can withstand before it strikes back.

"May you all be the posts with which my magic rattles!" I spat the words at them, and a flash of power swept over us all.

The shout was one of anger and hurt from deep inside me, and even its true meaning was unknown to me until the shouting ceased and strangled gasps began to gurgle up from low inside each one of the boys. Their eyes widened with confused horror as fingers clawed at their faces and chests, something transpiring within that was not yet evident on the outside.

"*Donnerwetter!* Rumpel, what have you done?" Lina shrieked in horror.

I had no words for Lina, and instead, I stood there watching in absent curiosity as the three boys eventually, quite literally, took root. Their booted feet sunk into the ground, as from the inside out they transformed into human-shaped wooden posts, flesh hardening and splitting like an aged tree trunk shaved of its bark, shocked expressions trapped forevermore in a cast of a wooden pole buried deep into the earth. I had turned them into the very thing they had accused me of rattling.

Lina screamed, fingertips pressed into her cheeks until they were surrounded by points of white, and with a coldness that was turning my insides to emotionless ice, I turned from her.

"This silly little creature leaves you to the trolls."

She was still screaming in the field that had once been my haven and then became my torment as I walked away. I didn't bother to even look back before I disappeared into the woods. There had never really been anything true or real for me in this place, anyway. My disillusioned form kept going until I was long past that village, and far away from the hellish pit that was Klimn and Grolge's cave.

I didn't belong in the fields of Freudenshafen, and I didn't belong in the cave of the trolls. Perhaps I belonged nowhere, but it was well past time I left all of this behind and set out into the world to discover whether or not there truly was a place meant for me.

CHAPTER THREE

hey say when a man wanders the earth unceasingly, that it is not a place, but himself he is seeking, and that he can search his whole life through without ever seeing the truth of himself at the end of his days. Cast out by my own people, raised as little more than food in a hole deep within the earth, I had no way of defining the creature that stared back at me from the water's surface. I searched and I sought, but I did not find the answer to the question forever in the back of my mind. Instead, I found only more of the mortal world and the hunger and greed therein.

The more I learned of the human world outside of Freudenshafen, the more I learned of how I could control them and bend them to my means. Hope is a very strong motivator when it comes to humans, and so long as they see what they think is a way out—even if it is but a wisp of smoke—then they will keep fighting and buy into whatever tale you spin.

As I travelled, I practiced my wiles, and with each new interaction I honed this ability to play them until I barely had to use my magic in order to be given their food, their cloth-ing, and their gold. My magic had also grown and developed, and when I had no desire for games, I had learned to call food—and clothing—through the spaces in-between our world. I had no other person to call my own or to tie my life to, but neither was I bound in servitude and miserable obedience. Loneliness was a fair price to pay to be one's own master.

Along the way, I did think to step back into the world of magic to see if now that I was grown—though still small in stature and haggard in appearance—I would be accepted due to my cleverness and experience. I had, in my own way, created a different sort of trickery and magic that was uniquely mine own.

So I travelled for decades, exploring other kingdoms outside the one of my birth, hoping that now I could step back into the place I had been cast out from, and found instead that the snobbery which had been the cause of my abandonment was still very much alive and, indeed, universal.

Magical beings such as elves and fairies live for eons—sometimes indefinitely—if no harm befalls them. No one wanted to take in a young, deformed creature that would cast a dark shadow upon their legacy. It did not matter where I went, or whom I sought out, I was not welcomed by the ethereal beings who were formed in shapes of perfection and loveliness. I was reviled and shunned, not welcome in any part of the magical kingdom, unless it was with the other dredges that sought only blood and flesh.

Eventually, I made my way back to my homeland—if I were to be alone, better that it be in a land that I knew and understood.

It wasn't my intention to end up near the royal city of Potsdamburg, but when I found myself naught but a morning's ride outside its walls in the small village of Nedlitzin, I discovered I had no desire to leave.

Only but a small village, it was a prosperous one, filled with quaint shops that sold many wares: sweet-smelling bakeries filled to the roof with pastries and breads, milliners who sold beautifully trimmed hats and bonnets, tailors selling the latest fashions from abroad, and stores where your feet could be shod in all of the best leather. All of which received patronage from wealthy farmers who owned the surrounding fields.

Nedlitzin was also home to a successful merchant who gathered spices and oils in many lands and brought them to be sold in the King's City. Just as it hadn't been my intention to end up in this village, it also wasn't my intention to become ensnared by his household and all that took place within its walls. I found myself sneaking into the shadows left by the large towers and peeping through windows to watch his servants and handmaidens serve the young lady of the house.

Sweet Katrin, with locks of sunshine that curled about her blemish-free porcelain cheeks and eyes of bright jade, was a sight for any to behold, let alone a beauty-starved fiend such as myself. Though I had seen the finest of ladies around the world, there was some unspoken thing that continued to draw me back to her. Katrin's favourite place to spend her time was in the well-kept gardens behind their home, and there, in the shade of a large tree, she would sit upon a stone bench to read her afternoon away.

When she wasn't reading, she practiced her zither, preferring to do so outside with the breeze fluttering through her locks than to do so in the study of her home. Her fingers were so nimble and quick, plucking at the strings in a refined manner that seemed effortless, until music came spilling out. Occasionally, her honeyed voice would rise loud enough above the music that it would reach me in my place of concealment inside the bushes. Her voice was something that stayed with me even after she had ceased playing, finding me in my dreams and calling me awake from sleep.

I would watch her for hours, memorizing every little

nuance that seemed uniquely Katrin. The tilt of her head when she was truly enraptured by her reading, the way her lips tipped upwards at the corners when she was amused by the elderly gardener who told her tales of his childhood, and the way her eyes shone bright with happiness, but also grew pensive with emotion when she played, each habit and trait something that became written upon my mind and would never be forgotten.

I knew better than to allow yet another mortal girl take ahold of me, but something about sweet Katrin drew me in until I was the one be-spelled and enraptured. Perhaps it was the gentleness of her spirit, or how she treated even the scullery maid with respect and compassion, and though she loved her finer things—bright jewels and soft silken gowns— she never demanded of her merchant father anything. Instead, she accepted all gifts with a sweet gratefulness.

Her father, however, was a boastful man who took his claim to riches and power within the village seriously and believed that all others should, as well. He bragged of his many ships that sailed along the coasts, gathering all manner of fine things from other kingdoms and returning to port with treasures untold. He told tale after tale of his trips to the seacoast to check on his fleet and brought back proof of his self-proclaimed importance by brandishing exotic spices from kingdoms leagues and leagues away.

Despite the father raising her, Katrin seemed to remain unspoiled and it was his boasting that resulted in her imprisonment with the threat of death looming over head, no fault of her own. The human condition is a strange thing, when even men who have no need to make false claims because their lives are already so wondrous, still feel it necessary to falsify their truth in order to appear greater than what they are.

Such is what happened late one night at the local tavern,

when Moritz Friedrich claimed his lovely Katrin had the ability to spin straw into gold.

A drunken brawl broke out that night, as the truth of his wild tale was questioned. Come morning, once bruises and hangovers alike were nursed, and bloodied knuckles were bandaged, all seemed forgotten and life went on.

It was late in the summer, just on the cusp of fall when the afternoon breeze was beginning to chill, and the scent in the air promised night frosts to come. Word came of the approaching retinue—horse-drawn carriages surrounded by knights, and the royal banner flying high for all to see. King Ernst had come to the village in search of the girl who could weave straw into gold.

It would seem that the events of that night in the bar, though no longer spoken of, had not been forgotten, for it did not take long for the king's men to end up on the doorstep of the Friedrich household. Moritz's vanity was so fierce that he refused to confess the truth—that he had made up the tale of his daughter's ability—and instead allowed Katrin to be bundled up by her maids and handed off to the King's Guard.

I watched from behind a tree as the knights handed the beautiful girl up into one of the carriages, blonde head and full skirts disappearing inside while her family and the household watched. It all happened in a flurry of action, the king having come and gone before anyone had the chance to breathe. And while they all seemed content to remain motionless and let it happen, I was not.

Having no desire to get myself into Potsdamburg by means of my own feet, I snuck quickly beneath the legs of one of the large horses, sending it into a bucking fit that caused its rider to nearly go flying, and then crawled up to cling on beneath the nearest carriage, using my magic to keep myself latched on in a small hammock of fabric. I swayed back and forth beneath the carriage, the sound of clapping hooves upon the worn dirt roads eventually turning into the clack of horseshoes on cobblestone.

Potsdamburg was a city worthy of its king. Wide, stone streets filled to the brim with its citizens, all bustling and harried to get to their next location. The tall brick and stone buildings that towered over the merchants hawking their wares on the sidewalks were filled with glass windows and covered with scrolling, gold-carved cornices, braced beneath proud roofs sporting dentil moulding and lace trims. It spoke of health and prosperity...of a king who knew how to keep his kingdom strong and its pockets filled with coin.

The city proper paled in comparison to the king's palace. The lush, green gardens began long before one reached the seemingly endless granite steps that led up to the bright, sprawling home of the king. As one neared the palace, the gardens began to break into tiered levels, the steps splitting them down the centre. Each level contained its own intricate landscape of trees and bushes, leading up to a brick wall that rose up to begin the next level, its rooftop the floor of the next garden tier above. Windowed doors sprouted from the sides of each wall throughout the gardens, giving place for leafy grapevines to take root and creep up and over.

We did not travel by way of the staircase. Instead, the carriages moved freely up a winding cobblestone road to the main doors of the palace. Hammondburg Palace, set against the green of the hill, was a bright spot of canary yellow fighting the sun for prominence. It boasted columns of sand-stone that were carved into statues of Bacchants—a toast to life, love, song and drink.

As the king's retinue came to a halt outside the tall, proud doors of Hammondburg, I watched and waited.

First, the footmen jumped down off the back of the carriage where they had been holding on, their golden uniforms proclaiming them a part of the king's employ. They rolled out a carpet that led from the carriage to the main steps, trailing up to the now-open doors. One then placed a step at the foot of the carriage. One opened the door for His Royal Highness, King Ernst, who took the offered hand and stepped down out of his carriage and quickly made his way over the carpet and up into the palace.

Once he disappeared with only the barked command to "Bring the girl!" the doors were opened to Katrin's carriage, and I felt it sway above me as she and her guard moved inside, then climbed down. This time as I walked out amongst them, I cast a spell of overlooking, one that essentially made me invisible as it turned all eyes from me. It kept the horses quiet and meant that I was able to follow the guards as they took Katrin inside.

We travelled down numerous hallways and up several flights of stairs, until she was lead through a door and into a stone room with naught but a bed, one single window, a spinning wheel with stool, and heaps upon heaps of straw.

Not wishing to reveal myself yet, I slipped into one of the darkened corners to watch whatever would unfold between Katrin and the king—mostly to see just how the young, blonde beauty would handle this new development in her life. Either she had wept all of her tears in the carriage ride here or she had not yet come to fully understand the predicament she was in, for she took but a casual look around her, then moved to stand at the window gazing out from the tower to the gardens below.

"What have you gotten me into, Father?"

Or perhaps she did have an idea of what lay before her in this room, with its locked door behind us and barred window. Her slender fingers reached out to curve around one bar as she peered outside, possibly looking at what it was she was saying goodbye to. For a while, she stood there simply gazing out the window, and then at last she moved to seat herself on the edge of the bed, arranging her skirts neatly.

Still, I said nothing.

It was just as the sun was beginning to set in the sky, that the door unlocked, and servants entered, first to light the torches on the walls, and then stepped out, so that the king himself could enter instead. Katrin came instantly to her feet, with her skirts in hand, performing a graceful curtsy.

"Your Highness," she gasped out softly, startled and breathless.

"There are strange things being whispered about you in the taverns of Nedlitzin."

"Strange things, Your Grace?" Katrin gazed up from her curtsied position, a question upon her face.

"Yes, many strange and wondrous things." With his hand, he motioned for her to rise, his eyes taking her in as she did so, curious and assessing. "How old are you?"

"I've just turned sixteen years, Your Grace."

"Sixteen years," he murmured, reaching out with his hand to pluck a piece of straw from the large pile nearest him. "Sixteen years, and you shall die at dawn if this straw around us is not spun into gold by then."

Katrin was not the only one to startle at these words. I, too, gave a little jerk of my head as I looked between them quickly. The girl had paled, her green eyes wide in her face with a shocked innocence that did not quite comprehend what was being said.

"Your Grace?"

"Your father has boasted loud enough in Nedlitzin that it has made its way to my own ears that you have the most magical ability to spin straw into gold. I have brought you here to do that to all of this." His bejewelled hand swept out, motioning to the room at large.

"But, Your Grace, I can't," Katrin gasped out.

"Are you saying that your father is a liar?" The king was giving her a shrewd look, one that said one way or the other a member of the Friedrich family would be losing their heads come dawn.

"What? No, of course not."

"Then do this, or at dawn I will behead you." King Ernst's eyes glinted, dark and dangerous. Turning quickly on his heel, he slipped from the room, leaving the young girl alone amidst the straw piles.

Katrin collapsed to the floor in a heap of skirts, her clasped hands clutched to her chest as she gazed in despair at the straw all around her.

What had her father gotten her into, indeed?

CHAPTER FOUR

It was well within my power and ability to ease Katrin's fear of dying, and though I planned to go to her with an offer, it was not my intention to do so right from the start. Instead, I wished to see in what way she would handle this news. Would her despair take her over and have her clutching at her head to tear the hair loose? Would she cry until there was naught left in her but dry hiccups and ragged breaths? Or would she move to take up her perch on the bed, same as before, and simply await her coming death?

She did none of these, as it would turn out.

Standing tall, with her back straight and her shoulders squared, Katrin began to circle the room. Not bowed down by her hopeless fate, as her fingers brushed over strands of straw, she totalled the entirety of the room. It was impressive to see—her grace under such daunting odds—giving me a little more respect for the golden-headed girl I had been watching for months now.

With interest, I watched as she took up a small bundle in her arms and moved over to the spinning wheel. There was a determination in her look I could appreciate in the face of such impossibility, and I moved a little closer to have a better look as strands of straw were pulled from the small bundle now resting in her lap. Pressing her foot to the treadle, she began to work the straw onto the wheel as her foot pressed the treadle to make it begin to spin.

Of course, nothing happened, unable to even get the straw to stay together on the wheel such as wool would, and yet she tried over and over again until, at last, her shoulders slumped in defeat and she hung her head. I waited until her hands were over her face and her shoulders were trembling with quiet cries before I left my hiding place and moved towards her.

"You seem to be in quite the predicament, my dear."

My voice startled her, and she jumped a little on her stool. Her head popped up and tear-filled eyes gazed at me in confusion, quickly transitioning to mild horror.

"Who...who—?"

"Who am I?" I brushed a hand over my coif of pale hair that was pulled back off my face and tied at the base of my neck with a deep blue ribbon. The way I wore it caused my long, pointed ears to stand out all the more, but I was no longer averse to my appearance. Young in years as I may still be, I had come to accept the notion that I was as I was and there was naught to be done about it. Not all the magic in the world could change that. "I am a concerned citizen."

"Are you here to harm me?" Her voice quavered with a newfound fear as she continued to look at me, the foreign creature before her.

I laughed a short, dark chuckle at this question. "No, I am not here to harm you. Rather, I would like to make you an offer." I picked up a piece of straw, holding the end between a thumb and finger while pulling it through the other set of thumb and finger.

"What sort of offer?"

Tossing aside the straw piece, I pulled a small red handkerchief from the breast pocket of my little jacket and stepped towards her, offering the piece of cloth for her to dry her eyes. "The sort of offer that will save your life."

"How?" With trembling fingers, she reached out to take the handkerchief, and wiped her eyes with dainty dabs.

"I will spin all of the straw in this room into gold for you in exchange—"

"In exchange for what?" Her body straightened in resistance and she pulled back further on her stool, the hand around the red cloth tightening.

My hand rose to put a stop to the thoughts currently running rampant in her mind. "Not anything of that sort, dear one. No, I want the locket that you wear around your lovely neck."

This seemed to surprise her, and her hand lifted to wrap about the golden locket in a defensive gesture, as if I might reach forward and tear it from her.

"But this has no value to anyone but me."

"Well...not quite true. The gold is worth a pretty penny, but more importantly, I want it because of the value it has to you."

It was a delicately crafted piece—all filigree flowers making up the lid to it, allowing just a hint of what lay beneath to be seen through the gold work. Once one opened it up, they were able to see the tiny round coriander seeds and small dried blooms contained behind the pane of glass.

It had been a gift from her father, seeds from the very first ship he sent out across the sea to gather spices, herbs and oils to sell back here. I had heard firsthand Moritz telling the story to Katrin, of how these seeds had been of the first handful gathered for the voyage, and he'd put them aside for safe keeping. The blooms had come off the first successfully cultivated plant in their own garden, grown from seeds that had been in that handful. Now she bore them all around her neck, carrying the sweet memory of her father's first success, and she one of his most lovely treasures since.

I wanted the necklace not because of its monetary value,

but because of the familial meaning behind it, because there was so much of their pride in their name and their power wrapped up in that little gold locket.

She was hesitant, I could see, her eyes narrowed at my admittance of why I wanted it and the words of refusal were upon her lips, formed there in the pursing of her mouth while her fingers remained tight about it.

"Think carefully before you refuse—it is the locket or your head. Either way, the piece will not be staying around your neck."

A visible shudder made its way through her body at my words, and I watched the emotions play across her face. She was a prisoner of the king, there was nothing else she could do but hope that the little goblin-creature before her was actually capable of what he said.

"I want proof first."

Her words made me smile and feel a little proud of her. Even during these desperate times, she was not fool enough to take me at my word. I simply bowed my head in acceptance.

"My Lady." I gestured to the stool, signalling the need for her to rise so that I might take her place. "If you would be so kind."

Katrin was quick to hop up from the stool as I stepped near her, the rustle of her skirts adding to the sound of her hurried footsteps across the wooden floors. With a touch of dramatics, I flung out the tails of my coat and sat upon the stool. Pulling the stool up a little, I leaned forward to check on the wheel before me. The bobbin was already slid into place on the flyer and I reached out with my fingers to check that the whorl was set. My fingers travelled along the drive band that led from the wheel down over the bobbin and whorl. It seemed adequately taut, and I slid it into the proper position on both. I moved my foot to the treadle and worked it up and down, watching the bobbin spin freely inside of the flyer, and I knew that I was set to begin.

"Would you bring me the blanket from your bed?"

I was given a suspicious look at this request, but eventually she complied, and picking it up, brought it over to me.

Of course, she stopped far enough away that we both had to stretch in order for me to take it from her hand, and I offered her a pointed look in return. She wasn't winning me over with this behaviour, and of anyone, I was in the best position to help her—something her father certainly hadn't done by allowing her to be carted off, rather than confess to his lies.

Once I had the blanket, however, I paid her no heed. Picking at the edge of the knitted piece, I was able to get a loose strand of thread and pulled a length of it free. Snapping it off with my teeth, I threw the blanket back across the cell to land haphazardly onto the bed. From the corner of my eye, I saw Katrin move to pick it up, fold it, and then lay it back upon the end of the bed. Perhaps she was just looking for something to keep her hands busy. I didn't care.

With thread in hand, I looped it around the bobbin and ran it along the guide hooks before feeding it through the orifice at the end. Once all was set, my foot worked the treadle yet again as I tested the pull of the bobbin, which needed only a little adjusting of the tensioning screw down below.

Still ignoring Katrin, I leaned down and picked up the little bundle of straw that had fallen from her lap in her rush to flee from my approach. Pulling strands free, I looped the thread around the ends of it, and whispered words of magic to the straw in my hands, telling it to bind to the thread. As my foot worked, and the treadle rocked up and down, the wheel spun.

The cell was filled with the creek of the wooden spinning

wheel, and I could feel Katrin's eyes upon me as straw went into one side of the orifice and came out the other as a string of gold thread to be wound around the bobbin within the flyer. After I had done a couple of lengths, my foot paused, and I reached out to stop the wheel from spinning any further.

"Is that enough proof for you?" I asked her, turning on my little stool to gaze at her, a brow raised over one dark eye, mocking her earlier disbelief.

Katrin stepped slowly towards me, her eyes firmly latched on the bobbin and as if unable to help herself, she reached out to brush her fingertips along the golden thread wound about it.

"It truly is gold, isn't it?"

I simply nodded at her words, my eyes staying on her face.

There were so many emotions working over her features once again—disbelief, awe, but most of all, relief. Without further hesitation, her hands reached for the chain about her neck and she carefully lifted it up and over her head. Turning to face me, perhaps meeting my eyes for the first time since I had revealed myself, she held the locket out to me.

"We have a deal."

"Good decision."

I took the locket from her, and just to prove a point, slipped it over my own head and then dropped it inside my shirt so that it would rest against my heart, a medal of my victory in this moment. I had taken a prized possession, but she would keep her head.

"Now go away, I have work to do," I demanded, brushing her off as I set out to spin the heaps and heaps of straw within this room into gold for a man that had not earned it, and likely did not need it.

Katrin backed away, moving across the room to settle

upon the bed with her skirts arranged neatly around her and her hands clasped in her lap. I felt her eyes upon me as I worked, and though I wasn't keen on how those tables had turned, I dealt with it for the time being. Hours trickled by while I sat there at the spinning wheel, oftentimes only the creak of the wheel itself and the soft whirl of the flyer making any sound in the room. Periodically, I would change the position of the thread along the guide hooks to fill up other portions of the bobbin, and once it was filled, I would set it aside to be replaced with a fresh bobbin from the stack empty and waiting at my feet.

The work was unceasing, and even for a magical being such as myself, it took a toll on my body. Yet, I did not stop until every last piece of straw within the room had been spun into gold, adding to the pile of filled bobbins on the floor.

It was just before dawn when the wheel stopped spinning for the final time and I dropped my hands to my lap. Twisting my shoulders a little to pop an aching place in my spine, I then stood up.

"As promised, one room of straw spun into gold."

Surprisingly, Katrin had not fallen asleep the entire time, though there had been a couple of moments during the night when the soft noises of the wheel seemed to almost lull her, and I thought she would nod off. Instead, she had taken those times as a sign to move to the window for fresh air and gazed out over the darkened kingdom below. Though she wasn't doing the work herself, it had seemed she wanted to see it through to the end.

"Thank you for what you have done for me. You have saved my life."

"Nonsense. We had a deal, and I always keep my word." I patted the locket resting beneath the linen of my shirt and jacket.

A silence fell between us, during which I gazed around

the room, checking each crevice and corner for a stray piece. I saw none.

"Dawn is fast approaching and your king will return. Sleep while you can, my Lady."

I gave her a bow, more for the dramatics of it than to pay any respect. As I did so, I backed up until I was in the shadows and able to call up my spell to hide myself from view.

Katrin gasped as I disappeared, looking around her to see if I might have moved quickly into another area of the room. When she could find me nowhere, she sighed, pressing a hand to her cheek as she dropped down onto the edge of her bed to sit and wait.

Soon, the king would return, and his judgment of her fate would be made. As for me, I settled down into a corner to rest for the time being. I would be there to see King Ernst's thoughts on his findings.

CHAPTER FIVE

The king's reaction did not live up to anticipation.

Just shortly after sunrise, there was the scrape of a key in the lock and the heavy wooden door to the cell groaned open. Two of the King's Guard entered the room first, with King Ernst coming just shortly afterwards. Once again, Katrin stood to her feet at his appearance and offered a curtsy.

Not even sparing her a glance, his dark brown eyes swept the room over and finished up on the spinning wheel with its stack of bobbins beside it on the floor.

From the shadows, I watched the king cross the floor so that he might stoop down and pick up one of the bobbins. The newly dawned sunshine filtering through the window glinted off the gold thread wound smoothly around the piece, and he twisted it back and forth so that he could watch the sun play across it.

"So, he spoke true."

Katrin didn't respond, she simply remained standing there silently with her hands clasped before her. Her eyes followed him though, watching as he walked casually around the room with the bobbin of gold thread in his hand.

"See she is fed," he said to his guards, and then walked quickly to the door. "And collect those bobbins and bring them to me." The king's dark head of hair and broad shoulders disappeared outside the cell.

The tallest of the guards stepped forward to gather up the bobbins. Soon enough, they, too, were gone, and Katrin was alone in the room once more. I watched her shoulders slacken with relief as she dropped down on the bed.

Katrin was left there for some time. Her body and fortitude eventually gave out on her and I watched as she curled up on the small straw filled mattress and fell asleep.

While I waited along with her, curious as to what His Highness would choose to do with her now that the deed had been done, I called forth food for myself—a trick I had developed while travelling the world over, and which I found to be much easier than talking someone out of their food. I thought about the kitchens down below and pulled some cheese and a leg of duck through the space between and into my awaiting hands. The cheese was rich and fragrant. I nipped it down in large bites before turning to the juicy duck leg. It would seem there were some benefits to residing within the king's home.

I had eaten the bone clean by the time the cell door opened once more, and a servant girl entered with a tray of food and wine for Katrin. She woke in a groggy state, fingers rubbing at her eyes as she sat and fought to gather her bearings. The girl didn't say much. Instead, she set the tray at Katrin's side on the bed then fled quickly as if she might be attacked if she stayed longer than what was necessary.

What did they say in the palace below about the girl locked upstairs?

With careful movements that spoke of her groggy mind, Katrin picked up a piece of bread on the tray as well as the bowl of stew they had brought her and began to carefully eat. Even locked away in a cell she was still a lady of substance and grace.

Having set aside my own crumbs, I watched her as she ate —the small bites, the slow chewing, the way she did everything neatly despite the fact she had no idea there was an audience.

Once she had eaten her fill and washed it down with some wine, Katrin placed the tray on the floor, curling back up to sleep a little more. It was perhaps just past the dinner hour when the door was opened once more and Katrin was woken from her sleep by two guards who came to gather her.

"Am I going home?" she asked, her blonde hair in disarray from her sleep and her cheek still red from where it had lain upon her hand.

"The king wishes for us to take you elsewhere."

"What? Where elsewhere? Where are you taking me?"

Watching this unfold with interest, I stood to my feet, brushing my hands along my trousers to clean away any dust. Katrin was close to weeping as they pulled her from the room, and I was able to easily follow behind them entirely unnoticed.

We didn't have far to go before we were in yet another cell, this one larger than the last, and also filled to the brim with piles of straw. In the centre of this room sat a spinning wheel accompanied by a stool, and beside them, was set a pile of empty bobbins waiting expectantly.

So, it was to be assumed that the same request was going to be made of her that night as had been made the night before. The remainder of Katrin's questions went unanswered as she was left in the new cell and the door locked behind the guards. The girl stood in the middle of the room, an entirely new look of horror upon her features as it became clearer to her that thanks to my actions, the king believed her truly capable of spinning gold, and with no way of contacting me, she would not be able to give the king what he so very much longed for.

King Ernst, it appeared, had a keen sense of timing, for just when her horror had settled enough to make Katrin truly distraught, did the click of the lock sound and His Grace stepped into the room. Her legs failed her, and no curtsy came. This time the king was greeted with nothing but the bow of her head.

"How are you finding your new lodgings?"

"I thought...I thought I would get to go home."

"Until I am done with you, you are home," the king responded. His hands came to rest upon his hips as he gazed about the room like a man surveying a newly acquired piece of land. Pride and victory shone within the depths of his eyes.

Katrin remained quiet, as there was not much to be said in opposition to the king.

"It is my desire that you once again spin the straw before you into gold." He looked to the ashen-faced girl wringing her hands before her skirts. "And if you do not, I will have your head instead."

He had not even left the room this time before she dropped down to the hard, little bed in the corner, her face buried in her hands. "Please...oh please."

I decided to be kinder this time. More time would only make her more distraught, not desperate, and I had no desire to sit in the shadows listening to her sobbing when instead I could be moving forward with the great deal of work that I had to do. Leaving the shadows, I came to stand before her once again.

"Was that *please* for myself, or for the king?" I questioned, my eyes upon my nails as I picked at a hangnail that had formed during the hours of my work the previous night.

Katrin gasped, her head lifted free of her hands to gaze up at me, green eyes wide with surprise and a newly forming glee.

"You've come back! But...how?" She glanced about,

looking for the evidence of my miraculous entrance into the room somewhere in the corners.

"I have my ways. You've been crying. Why?"

"Because, though what you did for me last night was kind, the king wants it to be done again. Only now there is more, and I am still unable to spin gold from straw."

"Hmmm," I murmured, tapping a finger to my lips. "You do appear to be in quite the bind once more, don't you?"

"Will you help me again kind, little Sir?"

I glared at her a little as she referred to me as little sir. I was more than aware of my diminutive stature, there was no need to vocalize it.

"Your ring."

"Pardon?"

"I will spin the straw once more in exchange for the ring upon your hand."

We both looked down to her right hand where a large square-cut ruby rested upon her slender finger.

The ring was yet another piece that she never took off, a remembrance of her deceased mother who had left her when she was but a young girl. The ring had been the piece Moritz had used to propose to Aline all those years before. Shortly before Aline Friedrich's passing, she had removed it from her own hand to slide it into the small palm of her daughter, telling her to wear it for her, always.

Katrin's right hand clenched into a tight fist while her other hand came to cover the ring over. Looking up to her face, I saw the way her bottom lip trembled with unshed tears and unspoken words. She did not want to part with it, even less than she had wanted to give up her locket—but that was why I wanted it so greatly.

"Very well."

The next action took some effort on her part and I watched as her chest swelled, and her shoulders raised with a deep breath that seemed to help her in tugging the ring off her finger. The hand that held it out to me, palm up, with the red jewel gleaming upon it, trembled with emotion. It was a tender sight, and would have moved me, had I felt any remorse in removing this piece from her life.

Mortals were better off without their attachments to small, insignificant items. Pieces that could easily be taken or lost and yet made their whole world crumble as if they embodied the memory or the soul of the person they were meant to represent. The only thing that truly mattered was the length of our memory and what we held onto within us concerning a particular person—what they had been to us or what they had done. Upon my soul, I bore the marks of all those I had revealed myself to. I remembered each glance, every shudder, and all the sharp inhales of horror.

I did not require the aid of a piece of jewelry to carry those things with me, nor did Katrin need this ring to take the memory of her mother with her throughout her life. She would be better, stronger, if she chose not to carry her heart on her hand, but instead kept it safe within herself where no one could take it.

Without hesitation, I reached out and took the ring from her hand. Lifting it up between thumb and finger, I angled it back and forth to watch the sunlight reflect off the surface of the red stone. It was a beautiful piece, befitting a Lady, not just the wife or daughter of a merchant.

I slid it onto my finger, letting it wink its presence upon my index so that it would be there with every gesture and motion.

Our deal struck, I turned from her, and took up my seat upon the stool before the new spinning wheel. My actions were similar to the night before as I checked it over, except that this time, Katrin brought me the thread without me having to ask. I nodded an absent 'thank you' to her and then continued on with the process.

The room had almost doubled in size, which meant that the amount of straw I needed to spin in the same amount of time was a great deal more. It would require faster work and a lot more magic than had been necessary the previous night. It was, however, not a deed I was unsuited to—I worked best against the odds.

This time, Katrin paced, unable to sit still and simply watch as the night wore on. The straw piles diminished in a steady manner, but to anyone on the outside looking in, it looked like there might be some doubt whether or not the task could be accomplished in the time allotted. I was not fearful of the outcome, but then it was not my head at risk of the chopping block.

To her credit, she did not utter any of this doubt or dismay and left me to my work, choosing to express her worry in the steady pacing around the room. The annoyance of it eventually grated on my nerves, however, and I grumbled my irritation.

"If you need something to do, be of help and bring me each new bundle of straw when I run low, but do stop that incessant pacing before I go mad."

From that point on, the evening passed far smoother and with less annoyance felt on my part. When at last the final bobbin was filled, and I was able to cease my work and stand, the sun was still an hour from rising. I stood up and stretched out my back before turning to Katrin, who by this point had taken a more relaxed pose on her bed.

"The task is once again complete, my Lady, and you may rest easy." My bejewelled hand motioned to the bed, indicating that she should lie down and sleep. "Your life is safe for one more morning. May the king's greed not require more of you."

Katrin didn't speak this time. Conflicting emotions fought for prominence in her eyes and I don't think that she was capable of forming words in that moment. I saw relief that the deed was finished, perhaps a little thankfulness for my aid, but also hate for my demands, and fear for what the morning would actually bring.

Without another word, I slipped from her view and into the shadows.

This time, however, I did not stay in the room, but opened a hole in the wall through the space in between and stepped through, out into the hall. My curious nature was getting to me, and I wished to investigate what actually was on the horizon. It didn't take me long to find the answer to my question, for down at the end of the corridor was a bigger room—a bigger room with triple the amount of straw.

The king's greed was not yet at an end.

CHAPTER SIX

he king did not deign to grace Katrin with his presence this time around.

I was there in the wee hours of dawn to watch his guards enter the cell, and gather up the numerous bobbins of golden thread, leaving the girl with little more than a glance from their eyes.

It left her fearful, and instead of returning to sleep, she drew her legs up to her chest to sit huddled on the bed. Her position did not change when the servant girl entered to bring her meal. Instead, she sat staring at the spinning wheel in the centre of the room—a symbol of her imprisonment, and a hateful reminder of a fate which was no longer within her own hands, but held in the greedy, uncaring clutch of a man grown cold from his own power.

I would have liked to question her then, to understand what was truly going on inside her mind—but that would have broken the ruse that I left between visits, and I did not want her aware that I was present for all the happenings taking place inside these walls. I remained silent in the wings, watching the fear crawl beneath her skin until it was almost a tangible presence in the room with us.

She startled when the door eventually opened and the guards returned to fetch her once more.

I was fully aware of where they were taking her and what awaited her at the end of the corridor—another room, more straw, and another threat of beheading—but what was there left for her to give me in exchange for spinning? This had been the thought milling in my mind over the course of the morning.

"Please, I can't keep doing this! I simply want to go home. Will you speak to the king for me?" It was sad to see a proud young woman brought so low that she clutched at the sleeve of a guard and begged for his aid in dealing with the king.

She appealed to the wrong man, however. The guards were nothing more than puppets whose strings were pulled and plucked by His Grace. Shaken off with little thought, Katrin was left alone yet again, in a larger room with even more straw.

The door had no sooner shut, than it opened once more. Instead of a servant or even the king, Moritz Friedrich stepped into the room, his leather boots clicking on the wood beneath them.

"Papa?" came Katrin's shocked exclamation and then she launched herself into his awaiting arms. Her face was buried into the crook of his neck and shoulder.

I watched as the girl sobbed, clutching onto the form of her father to ensure he was not going to leave her any time too soon. In return, Moritz held his daughter tightly, his arms about her slender form and his own face pressed to the top of her head.

"What are you doing here? I wanted so badly to see you...but I wanted to go home. Are you now their prisoner as well?" Finally, she lifted her tear-streaked face to gaze up at her father, distraught at this new thought.

Moritz, in a calming manner, lifted his hands to cup her face between them, smoothing away her tears with his thumbs.

"I am not a prisoner, and neither are you." His words brought a frown to her face.

"But—"

"Katrin, do you not realize what you have done for us? I spoke what I thought were drunken words of falsehood when I boasted of your abilities in the bar that night, but I had no idea it was the truth! Why didn't you ever speak of this to me?"

"No, Papa, I haven't—"

Moritz was not truly listening to her, too swept away by the possibilities that arose with this new talent.

"But you have, and you will again." He nodded firmly, eyeing her with determination.

"You don't understand. I can't do this, I haven't any more to give."

"Well, you must find it. Whatever has given you this magical ability, you must find it again. You will be queen, my darling."

"What?" This time Katrin froze, and I watched the way her eyes widened with this announcement.

"The king called me here to the palace to speak with me. If you do as he asks and spin this final room into gold thread for him, he will make you his queen. Queen Katrin! Think of what you can do for your family—what pride and accomplishment you've brought us. Do this and all will all be ours —a throne for you, and my grandsons will rule this land."

I could see the thoughts racing through her mind, the way she paused to contemplate his words. Could she want this, to marry the man who had pulled her from her home at but a moment's notice, and left her locked away for three days now—the man who had now threatened her life not once, but twice? It seemed, even to me, a ghastly and humiliating thing to ask of the girl.

"I don't know that I can."

His hands tightened upon her face, and he angled her chin up so that he could lean in closer, his eyes firm upon hers. "You must. As a family, we need this and there is little alternative. Do whatever you must to give the king what he asks, do you understand me?"

Such is a father's love.

Katrin nodded her head subtly. "Yes, Papa."

"I love you." Moritz pressed a kiss to her forehead, then released her, and stepped back. "I must go now; they didn't give me much time. I have faith in you, Katrin. I know that you can do this."

His steps had taken him to the door, and he rapped upon it with his knuckles. Katrin was shaking again, her hands clasped before her, turning white as she watched the door open to her father, and his form step through it.

"I love you, Katrin," he repeated. "Make me proud."

The door closed on his words, and yet again, it was only the two of us alone in the room. I wondered if this would be the end of it—would they leave her to her work, or would the king manage to show himself?

This question seemed to be upon Katrin's mind as well, for as she sat down, there remained a strained tension in her body. She looked to be waiting for something, or someone.

We did not have long to wait.

King Ernst entered the room in a flourish of capes and jewels, filling up the room with his presence. Katrin, who I had half-expected to simply remain seated this time, stood to her feet, and offered the king a full curtsy once again, followed by a softly murmured, "Your Grace."

"Your father was here, and I presume he has told you the offer that I have made?" He swept his cape aside and rested a hand on his hip as he gazed at her.

"Yes, Your Grace, he has."

The king nodded his head, jaw set with intent and a grand purpose that I was sure made all the sense in the world to him—justifying your actions comes very easily when there is no one who can oppose them. King Ernst strode towards Katrin and took her pale hands into his own, clasping them in the manner of an intimate lover.

"Then you know I plan to make you my bride, my queen." I watched him release one of her hands so that he could reach up and gently tuck a strand of her hair behind her ear. "I ask only one thing from you."

Katrin was spellbound, whether from pleasure or from terror, I could not be certain—but the display made my own stomach roll. There were a few choice words tossing about in my head that I would use to describe His Royal Highness, and none of them were regal.

"Nothing more than I have asked of you before. Show how true your love for me is by spinning the straw in this room into gold thread and in the morning, I will announce our betrothal."

The only response Katrin seemed to have for this was a subtle nod of her head, though her skin had taken on a sickly pallor.

"You make me very happy in this, Katrin. You will make a beautiful, and dutiful wife."

"Thank you, Your Grace," she whispered to him.

"But I expect obedience. Know that, and if you should choose not to finish this room for whatever reason..." he said, his words drifting off deliberately. King Ernst shook his head, eyes levelled upon hers. "The outcome still stands, and instead of a wedding, there will be an execution."

If it was possible for the girl to turn whiter, it happened, and her eyes widened to a shocking size.

"And neither of us wants that, do we?" The tone he spoke to her in was condescending, turning her into a small child that needed to be spoken down to.

Slowly her head shook, concern creasing her pale brow. King Ernst was wholly unaffected by this obvious sign of outward distress and lifted her hands to his lips so that he could press a kiss to the curve of her knuckles. Her hands were then released, and he stepped back.

"You have a great deal to do. I will leave you to it. Do not disappoint me, Katrin."

Once again, the tread of boot steps crossing the floor sounded, and the heavy door was opened to allow the king to pass through into the hall.

After the loud click of the lock sliding into place echoed around the room, I leaned against the wall to wait. It would be interesting to see how long it took for her to crack this time.

She was a mess of emotions—that was easy to see. Her hands to her cheeks, Katrin sat down on the edge of the small cot, staring across the room at the spinning wheel with a sort of hatred and fear that I had rarely seen in someone's face.

"Friend....please come to me again," her plea was whispered softly, but I heard, it nonetheless.

I should perhaps have joined in on the speed at which things had been happening today, but I moved only on my own terms, and as she called to me, I contemplated. I would free her if she but asked me. I was certain there was a reasonable exchange we could settle on in return for me opening the wall and helping her slip out unseen.

I did not fear the anger of her father or even the king when the knowledge of her absence became known—but I needed her to speak the words for herself, to ask that she be freed from this upcoming marriage. That was how magic worked, and though I was free to do as I pleased, there was still a magical contract that formed during these exchanges. I gave magic in return for fair trade, but first the bargain had to be struck. Having settled on what I was willing to do, and at what cost, I slipped from the shadows into her view.

There was an expression of relief awaiting me in her gaze as her eyes landed upon me. I saw the release of a held breath and how some of the tension slackened from her form.

"You beckoned?" I commented, then began a slow trek around the room.

There really was an absurd amount of straw in the cell, and I was relieved to think that I wouldn't need to deal with all of it. She and I had been through this twice already, and I could have prodded her more to speak, or saved both of us the trouble and simply announced what was going to happen —but that was not how this worked.

"I need to beg your help one last time, though I have nothing to offer."

Once she asked to be released, I had a number of ideas in mind for what she could give me, of that I wasn't concerned.

"Let me make a guess, you wish for this room to also be spun into gold?" I said it expecting her to tell me no and ask for rescue instead.

"Yes."

"Excuse me?" I wasn't so sure I had heard her correctly.

"I need for you to spin this room into golden thread as you have the past two nights."

I gazed at her, a stupefied look upon my face.

"Are you certain? There is nothing else you wouldn't rather ask for?"

Katrin paused, words on the tip of her tongue, and I waited for her to gather her wits about her and ask for help in escaping.

"I think...I would very much like to be queen."

"What?"

I shouldn't have been surprised at the process of the human mind—or their ability to look past horrors to shiny new things—but there you have it, I was surprised. Shocked she would allow the man who had threatened her thrice now to take her as wife, all for the sake of a crown.

"I wish to be queen. I know I haven't anything to give you now, but the king has promised to make me his queen, and if you do this for me, I will have many things I can give to you."

"Of course, think of all the new gowns." I shook my head, disappointed in her.

I had come out here with a plan to set her free and already settled on what pieces in her home I would take as my payment. However, things had now changed. Instead of seeking her freedom, she was asking to be permanently chained to the black-hearted man who sat upon the throne.

I twisted on my foot, my fingers stroking along my chin as I contemplated what I would take. There was a spark in my dark green eyes as I spun back to her—a spark that was turning quickly into a fire.

"Very well. If it is queen you wish to be, then I will spin this straw once more for you and in exchange you will give me your firstborn child."

"What?" It was her turn to doubt that she was hearing correctly.

My eyes narrowed on her, and I could feel my lips forming a bit of a sneer as I stepped towards her. "I will spin this straw into gold once more so that you can keep your pretty head and marry your king. In return, I want to be given the firstborn child that is conceived through this marriage."

It was the one thing I could not acquire for myself, and if I were going to do this, that was my price.

"I can't...that is not something that I can promise." Katrin gasped, a hand at her throat as she stared at me with suspicion and horror.

I shook my head at her and moved to lounge on the stool. "Don't give me that look, I don't plan to eat it." Just to make a show of how at ease I was—it wasn't my neck on the line—I picked idly at a tooth with my pinky finger.

"But I can't give up my child."

"Of course you can, parents do it all the time." Mine had.

"But—"

"Do you want to die?"

"N-no."

"Then make this vow now, and I will spin this straw and hand you the crown. Then, upon the birth of your first child, I will return at sunset to claim it. You will give me the child without complaint or resistance."

Our eyes met across the expanse of the room. Warm sunshine filtered through the window to the left of me, heating the straw and filling the entire room with the strong scent of it.

Minutes ticked by, during which I am sure she weighed diamonds and tiaras against the love of a future child, or the idea of imminent death. At last, she settled something inside of herself and responded.

"Very well. If this is my only choice...spin the straw into gold and my firstborn is yours."

CHAPTER SEVEN

I left shortly after I finished spinning the mountainous volume of straw in the third room, offering little more than a nod of my head and a reminder of the pact we had made, before I disappeared into the shadows. This time, I did not stay to see how the king received the completed task, nor did I wait to see if a formal proposal would be made. I had seen more than even I wished to—of all of them—and it was my desire to leave the palace and distance myself from any more of it.

Just when I thought I had come to understand everything that there was of the human race, these last few days had occurred and opened my eyes to all new forms of disgust that was to be felt over them and their ways.

I removed myself from society, to the safety of my small cabin in the woods on the outskirts of Nedlitzin. It wasn't a grand affair, but for a home I had built for myself, it was pleasant enough. Cool in the summer, warm in the winter, with a roof that didn't leak, and floors that were dry, it was more than I had been given in the early years of my life—best of all, I had to share it with no one.

Though, as I thought of it, the little cabin I shared with only myself would need to be reworked if I were to be bringing a child into the home. I knew that it could be years, but I would need to be prepared. The small kitchen that was adequate enough for myself would not be suitable for me to prep meals for a human child. I would need to add cupboards, and a place for an ice chest to be installed. Perhaps another window would be of importance, as the space was a little darker than I had realized before. While I was used to a lack of sunshine, most humans seemed to enjoy a great deal of it in their places of habitation.

Of course, another bedroom would be necessary as well, a small room off of the warm living space where the stone fireplace was built into the wall. It was a happy little fireplace, with rocks I had hand-picked from the riverbed and stacked upon themselves until there was a mantle and chimney creeping up the wall. The cabin wasn't much, but I thought I could make it into a happy enough home for myself and the child I would be bringing to raise here.

As I had expected, it was only a matter of days before the announcement was spreading around the city and villages proper that the king was to be wed to a beautiful village girl from Nedlitzin who had performed miracles for His Highness. The villagers were ecstatic, and as I slipped back into the town, winding my way through back allies and down back streets until I was able to get into the places I needed, I listened to the talk in passing.

The fact that it was one of their own—not a lady of nobility, but a merchant's daughter—seemed to please the people. Katrin, it seemed, would be a queen of the people.

When the wedding finally happened, it was a monstrous affair—days of festivals and celebrations throughout the city. Her dress was an occasion all of its own. Yards of satin and lace had been imported from the far reaches of the globe, and with a train so long and heavy it required six handmaidens to carry it down the aisle for her. They were married in the cathedral as all royal wedded couples are, and once their holy vows were spoken, a carriage transported the king and his new queen throughout the city with a parade following in their wake. It was an ostentatious show of wealth and power that left everyone with something to say for weeks.

Against my better judgement, I was there, seated upon a sill in the clerestory to see the entire production. Watching as the large cathedral doors swung open to reveal Katrin in her ivory gown that paled in its beauty only when compared to her own. Her golden hair was caught up from her face in a large braided crown that made its way around her head and was woven with greenery and flowers. I had not seen anything as lovely as she was in that moment—young, fresh, and still filled with the new bloom of life that belongs to young women before they have come into their prime.

While the ceremony itself was long and dull, it was Katrin I remained focused on. She carried herself with a presence of mind that was impressive for someone of her age, and it was my thought that King Ernst might not break her in the end. Her voice rang steady and true as she repeated her vows, and there did not seem to be any hesitation in her actions as she stretched out her hand for him to slip the wedding band upon her finger. It would seem she had fully committed to this new position in life and was prepared to be the steadfast woman at his side who did not falter.

Queen of them all—thanks to gold thread she had not spun. Queen, thanks to a lie woven in the darkness of a tower cell.

I didn't stay to watch the days of feasting and drinking that followed. Extravagance and excess was a human trait that I did not need more proof of. Most creatures that live took only what they needed to survive, or what they needed to prepare for the coming winter when rations were low and food scarce. Humans, however, ate more than what they needed, then threw away the rest. They took more than was their fair share and saw nothing wrong with this bad habit.

King Ernst was the most guiltiest of this tendency.

Throwing celebrations that, while they brought pleasure to his people, wasted precious resources and sometimes left people without, once all was said and done.

After the exuberance of the wedding, and the celebrations that surrounded it, Postdamburg settled into a quiet state and winter fell upon the city. I remained in my small cabin in the woods outside Nedlitzin, steadily finishing things around the cabin that would make it more hospitable for a child, and also keeping an ear open for any news that an infant was to be expected.

Two years passed before the news came. It was early fall, and Katrin had just celebrated her eighteenth name day, when the cry went out through the Royal City and travelled to the outlying towns. The queen was with child—King Ernst would have an heir. Except the child wasn't meant to be his, the child was meant to be mine, and had been since that fateful day.

To ensure that my investment was being taken care of, and that Katrin remembered the promise she had made me, I ventured to the palace once again. As easily as a shadow, I traversed the hallways of the king and queen's home, passing servants with little concern.

Katrin had not yet begun her lying in, when I discovered her in a small personal room where she and her ladies-in-waiting sat stitching patterns onto linen pulled taught in wooden hoops.

She was not alone, though. Moritz had come to visit. Moritz, looking even wealthier than the last time I had seen him. Being the father-in-law of the king did wonders for a man's status.

Katrin looked pale, and as her father approached and knelt before her, she requested that all her handmaidens leave them for a private audience. Obediently, the women filed out until it was only Katrin and her father remaining.

"Father, I have urgent news that I need inform you of. The truth of how I spun the straw into gold and became queen, and what that has to do with my present state. It is the cause of my constant concern."

Moritz took her hand in his own and patted the top of it gently, while his other hand clasped it tenderly within his hold.

"How it was done no longer matters, Katrin, not when you are now queen."

Katrin leaned forward, grabbing both of his hands between her own and clinging to them tightly. Her gaze was intent upon him.

"But, Papa, it does. There was a little man with large, dark eyes and long, pointed ears, who came to me from the shadows like a house goblin. He told me that he could save me, that he could spin the straw, but made me give him first my locket in exchange. You know the one, with the coriander seeds? And the next night, it was Mother's ring." She held up her hand to show that it no longer bore that particular piece.

Her father was looking at her with concern and a dawning suspicion. I could tell that his thoughts were not going in the direction that Katrin was hoping.

"Kat..." His tone was chiding, wishing to stop her before she went farther.

"No, Papa, it's the truth. Both nights he spun the straw for me, that's how it happened. However, on the third night I had nothing to give him…. I had come here with only what was on me and Ernst wanted me to be his wife, and you did as well. So, I did what I had to. I *promised* what I had to."

Moritz was gazing at her uneasily, the spinning cogs in his mind visible, and I wondered what it was he thought she was going to say.

"Promised what?"

Instead of responding to his question verbally, Katrin

placed a hand over her stomach to signify the unborn child within. His eyes dropped, and Moritz visibly jerked backwards a little, then surged forward to grasp her upper arms.

"What have you done to the child, Katrin? What are you planning? That could be the king's heir. Whatever the voices are saying, you cannot do anything."

"Papa...no. I'm not—I'm not mad. I'm speaking the truth! There was a small, elfin creature that came to help me. You need to believe me, or he will come and take the baby once it's born."

I needed to see no more. It was clear that Katrin had not forgotten our pact, and that she was taking it seriously. As much as she might wish to get herself out of it, the magic of the vow was binding, and she would have to give me the child when I came to collect it.

The next few months passed without incident. I travelled into Nedlitzin when I was bored and wished to be entertained by the people there, all the while keeping my ears open for the birth we were all waiting on.

Occasionally, I pondered what excuse Katrin would use once the child was gone. Would she claim death, or perhaps, that the child had been stolen? It would be easier for all if she merely claimed the child had not survived its birthing.

They say that the young queen laboured all through the night to bring new life into the world and that King Ernst paced the halls outside his throne room as he awaited news of an heir. But the summer day was lovely, and the sun bright, when the bells tolled in the early morning air just after dawn to signal the birth of a new royal. The tolling was followed by the announcement that the queen had birthed a daughter—the Crown Princess of Germaine, Princess Imelda Leona Liese.

The king was wroth. The little princess was meant to be a prince and succeed him on the throne, an heir to confirm his legacy and carry on his bloodline. The queen had failed him in that respect, but I could not have been happier.

In my little cabin, a sweet little room had taken shape that I filled with freshly cut florals, and arranged with silks and satins ensorcelled from naive village people. Most importantly, the locket and ruby ring were protected in velvet boxes awaiting the moment when I could gift them to the little princess—to offer her a piece of her human life, and tell her of the woman who had born her, and given me the family that I could not achieve on my own.

For my kind, I was very young to be considering a family of my own. Due to the long, indefinite stretch of an elf's existence, it was most common to wait until after the age of adulthood had settled upon them before considering marriage and breeding. Most often, well into the first—if not second—century of life.

Yet for me, waiting for the age of adulthood to be upon me was not an option. Life had seen fit to finally reward me, to bring into my path the opportunity for a child, and I was meant to seize it now.

While a disappointment to Ernst, the princess would be my pride and joy, the first creature to come into my existence who loved me unconditionally—the daughter I would otherwise not be able to have. The king and queen might want to have a proven succession, but thrones and kingdoms were not of my concern, and I would build for myself the one thing I had always been denied. From out of this mess would come my family, and little Imelda would want for nothing. Of that, I would make certain.

I gave them until that evening before I made my appearance, slipping first into the small nursery where the babe was being kept and watched over by a wet nurse. I had already taken in a goat to aid in that part for me. Just as I had supped from goat's milk and grown strong, my child would, as well.

She was a sweet, cherub-cheeked creature—fresh white skin with the blush of new life beneath it, and a slight smattering of blonde curls upon her round head. Though she slept, she made soft smacking noises—dreaming of feedings to be had, and warm nuzzles.

Leaning over the bassinet, I brushed a knuckle along her silken cheek, and felt the stirring of something within my chest. An emotion that was swelling and spreading outwards to encompass me in my entirety.

"Soon, little one, and we'll go home."

Katrin was not sleeping when I found her—not like I had expected. It seemed that she had been waiting for me to appear, and as I slipped from the shadows, she sat upright in her bed. There was a bundle of blankets about Katrin's legs and in her grasp she had what appeared to be a letter opener.

"So, you have come," she murmured into the space between us.

My head nodded to the piece of metal in her clasp.

"You were expecting me, but just what is it you plan to do with that?"

"Whatever it is that I must to keep you from taking my daughter. I am surprised you've come here first, and not simply snuck off with her back to the shadows you dwell in."

"Above all else, I am a creature of honour. The deal was struck between you and I, therefore you must be the one to relinquish her."

"Then I shan't do it. You may not have her, I refuse."

Katrin's face had aged somewhat in the two years since our parting. She had the look of a girl grown into womanhood, and there was now a deeper understanding of the world and how it worked resting within her eyes.

Motherhood, I thought, had done a lot of that, and King Ernst the rest.

"And if that be the case, you will die."

"You will kill me then, to take what you want?" Her gaze was hardened upon my features.

"No, but the vow was of a magical nature, and it is binding. Unless you have magic to break it, it will claim your life to repay the debt owed, and I will take the child anyway."

"Debt." She spat out the word, a desperation filling the newfound tension in her form.

"Yes, debt. We had an arrangement and agreed on an exchange. That is how the magic was able to happen."

Her hands pressed to her face, and I thought perhaps she was trying her best not to cry.

"I am queen now… Please, take anything else but my daughter. I will give you anything else," she pleaded with me.

"I cannot. All the valuables in the land do not equal that of a human life."

Katrin flung aside her covers, and launched herself—staggering—from her large, four-poster bed, to land on her knees before me with hands raised upwards in a motion of begging.

"*Please?* I beg of you, there must be *something* that can be done instead?"

My dark eyes took her in, kneeling upon her knees. Her present height offered a few spare inches so that I now looked down upon her. I studied the stress-etched lines upon her face, which pain and fear had wrought, and knew that in some small way, I could ease her pain. Though it wasn't needful in the least—and it was well within my right to refuse her and claim the child for myself—I couldn't help but think of the sweet, innocent Katrin I had watched in her family home. The same, sweet Katrin, I would later tell Imelda of, and the way in which she had captivated me until I was forced to come forward to help her.

It was for that sweet girl of memory that I spoke.

"I can only offer but a chance," I warned her, my voice soft.

"Anything!"

"I will give you three different chances, on three different nights, to guess my name."

In a lot of ways, it was a trick in and of itself. My 'name' was naught but a cruel joke thrust upon me by cave trolls, rather than any true gift bestowed upon an infant—and there was not a soul left alive who knew it.

"If you should guess correctly, our debt shall be considered settled and the little princess will remain with you. However, if by the third night you have failed to guess, Imelda will leave with me as was intended." I paused to look down at her.

"Do I have any actual chance of succeeding?"

"Of course. So...do we have an agreement?"

"Yes." It was upon a pitiful breath that the agreement was released.

"Excellent, tonight we shall begin. Your first guess?"

Katrin didn't bother to move from her position. Instead, she sat back on her heels and peered up at me.

"Maurice?"

"No." One of my brows lifted towards her. "Tonight's second guess?"

This turn, she took a little more time to think about it, before issuing a name.

"Gustaf?"

"No." I raised my hand and produced three fingers to encourage her on towards her third name.

She sat there for some time, and her thoughts were so loud that I could almost see her going over each and every one of the men that she'd known in her lifetime, trying to imagine what names might be most suited to a tiny creature that visited her from the shadows.

"Klaus?"

I simply shook my head and turned from her, heading towards the darkened corner of the room.

"Better luck tomorrow night."

"You said I had a chance!"

I turned back to her, gazing somewhat over my shoulder, at the figure kneeling in despair in the centre of the room.

"You do, but there are a lot of names in the world, and you must choose only one."

CHAPTER EIGHT

I couldn't bring myself to feel sorry for her. Katrin had chosen her lot in life nearly three years earlier, when she asked that I turn the third room of straw into gold in exchange for her firstborn child so that she might become queen. She could have asked for anything in the world, but what she had wanted was to marry a greedy, cruel-hearted man, and wear his crown.

I slept well that night after I returned to my cabin in the woods, and rested easy all through the next day, for I had offered Katrin the glimpse of hope that she needed—though it was nothing but a poultice for an inevitable wound. Two more nights remained, but try and try as she might, Katrin would never guess my name.

It did offer me some form of amusement to ponder her behaviour today. Had she kept this to herself, or was she seeking the help of her ladies-in-waiting and any other person that happened into her room? What names would pass over her tongue the next evening when I returned?

It was with this curiosity, that I returned to the palace that night, slipping unheard through the halls. As I had the night before, I went first to the nursery, gazing down at the sleeping wonder that lay nestled inside the small bed.

This time, she woke, vivid blue eyes the colour of a crystal-clear lake on a summer day peering up at me. She didn't startle, nor did she cry. Rather, she looked up at me in a steady manner that pierced me straight through to my core and left me open and vulnerable.

"I will give you the world, Princess," I vowed softly, and brushed my fingers lightly over the top of her head.

The soft fuzz of curl felt like satin beneath my touch, and it made my heart hurt in a way I had not yet felt. There was a frailty and delicateness to this tiny form that I had not at first imagined.

Not allowing myself too much time spent in the nursery, I went to Katrin's chambers who—seated this time at a small table with a lamp burning in the centre of it—was waiting for me. On the table before her was a sheet of paper, upon its surface were a number of names listed, crossed out, and re-scribbled.

Katrin, it would seem, had been very busy.

"Good evening, Your Highness." I flourished a bow, only partially from a mocking spirit, and righted myself.

Katrin looked weary—the sign of her sleepless night worn there upon her face—which made me believe that she loved her daughter and had no desire to let her go. Promises made easily years earlier, before the weight of motherhood had settled upon her, were now weighing more heavily than she had anticipated. At sixteen, Katrin had not thought this would hurt as terribly as it did, at eighteen.

"I have no need for pleasantries. Ancel?"

Her features had never looked so fierce as they did that night. She had found a strength within her that, I think, caught both of us by surprise.

"I see we are getting straight to the point tonight," I murmured, and straightened the little forest-green jacket that I wore. "No, not Ancel."

Katrin's eyes dropped to the sheet of paper before her, fingers gliding down over the names listed, perhaps with the hope that the correct one would leap from the page towards her.

"Leander?"

I snorted softly, unable to help myself. "What mother would gift a child, with this god-awful face, such a fanciful name? No."

There was a tension building once more in her shoulders as the hopelessness of this cause became even more apparent with each wrong answer. She was quiet, seeming to be lost in thought, as she stared down at her list.

"Your third name, my Lady?"

"Clemens?" she whispered.

I could appreciate the irony—a name that meant merciful. She could only hope.

"No, that is also not my name."

I did not wait for any further exchange. Rather, I turned silently to slip out of the room.

It was a sign of my own hubris that I did not contemplate the desperation of a mother's love, or the extent to which one would go to protect her child. Having now spent years slipping in and out of this palace undetected, I no longer concerned myself with the thought of being seen, which was how I failed to take note of the figure following along behind me as I left the palace. Nor did I notice as it followed me on my way into Nedlitzin, before both of us disappeared into the woods.

It was late and, once again, I turned in for the night with strong confidence that the next evening would see me returning with the little princess so that we could begin our new life. I wasn't aware of the eyes watching me from the windows, or that they remained there in the bushes the whole night through.

Come morning, I was singing—the excitement and happiness within my form could not be contained. In just a few short hours, I would have the start to my very own dream. The one thing that had remained out of my grasp for all of these years would soon be mine. For tonight, I would acquire my own version of a family.

No one could love the little princess as I could—one who had been denied love all of his existence and had wanted nothing but. I would not wrong her, as the cave trolls had me, nor use her for my own gain. With me, Imelda would be honoured and cared for, which was more than I could say of her human father.

The day had proven just as happy as myself, mirroring the sunshine inside me with the brightness of its sky. In the heat of the day, I worked out in the yard, picking a large bouquet of wildflowers that grew naturally around the cabin. I filled the house with them, so that the scent that greeted us tonight would be warm and fresh, welcoming my daughter to her true home.

As I worked, I hummed, which turned into a tavern song I had once heard soldiers singing around a late-night fire. Eventually, the lyrics changed to ones of my own.

"Soon, soon, I'll bring you home, forever I shall be your cornerstone. And for me, you shall be the same, for they will never guess, that Rumpelstiltskin is my name."

I couldn't seem to contain myself, and like a small child I waltzed about the yard until my arms were full of flowers, continuing to sing my song to the animals of the woods. Once I had all that I could carry, I set to work scattering them around the cabin, and within the room Imelda would call her own.

That night, when I arrived at the palace, I did not stop first at the nursery—when I stepped into that room, I wanted to be able to pick her up and take her with me. Instead, I went straight to the queen's chambers, but found her not alone. This time, Moritz stood at her back, his hand resting upon her shoulder.

I gazed at the two of them in mild curiosity. Did they think that when she failed to guess my name, he would be able to overpower me, and stop me from taking the princess with me?

I also noted that Moritz did not startle as I appeared in the room, and I wondered when he had begun to believe his daughter's tales of the small goblin who'd come to help her. When last I had seen, he had thought her mad.

"I see that we have company this evening."

"Will that be an issue? He can leave." The hand upon her shoulder tightened, a silent comment that Moritz did not agree.

"No, your father may remain."

This comment did elicit a reaction from both of them.

Despite all that had happened, neither of them had expected me to know who Moritz was. Had I been meant to think that this aged man was the king, and that they were presenting a united front? I doubted highly that Ernst was at all aware the presence of his daughter in the palace was up for question.

Katrin nodded to my words and pulled her slip of paper towards herself. Were they the same names as had been there before, or had she replenished the list with fresh ideas?

"Your first guess?" I prodded. I was done with the charade and wished to be done with this, she'd had her chance, now I wanted to take my daughter home.

"Hamin?" she asked, after a show of contemplation.

"No. Your second guess?" My heart was beginning to hammer faster in my chest as the moment drew nearer.

There was a longer pause this time, both of us aware that this was the last and final night, that at the end of these guesses, she would have no more.

"Anatoly?"

Our eyes met across the room.

"Incorrect. Your final guess, Your Highness? And do take your time with this one," I taunted, with perhaps a sign of victory shining within my eyes.

Katrin however, had not given up, nor was she looking as defeated as I would have thought. Instead, there was a light of something growing in her own eyes, one that I could not place.

"Is your name....Rumpelstiltskin?"

"No—" Over the pounding of my own heart, thinking that her fate was now sealed, I almost didn't hear her, and was quick to state my dismissal of her guess. Only she hadn't guessed wrong, and there was triumph in her gaze, and a sick sort of victory gleaming in the eyes of Moritz. I shook my head in denial, because this was not possible.

"No?" Moritz asked, his tone telling me that he already knew the answer, and that somehow, I had been the one duped.

"How?" chokingly escaped me, as the tower of hope and happiness that had built up inside me over the past few days began to tumble and crash down around me in an earth-shattering way.

It shouldn't have been possible. It *wasn't* possible, but something had taken place that I didn't understand, and somehow the truth had been laid at Katrin's feet.

"Is it, or is it not, your name?" the queen demanded in a harsh, forcible tone, fingers taut upon the end of her armrest.

"Yes. It is my name."

I was desolate, lost to my own shock and grief. I paid no heed to their actions.

Moritz was almost upon me before my wits finally returned, and I realized that I was at risk of true harm—a knife was drawn and aimed for my heart.

"Not today!" I shouted at him, stomping my foot viciously against the floor.

The force of it rattled the entire room, and the cracking of stones sounded from beneath us as the stone tiles shattered and separated. Katrin gasped, and her father stumbled backwards, his knife clattering to the floor.

They had stolen everything from me in some rotten, foul, play-of-wits that I could not yet fathom, but I would not let them have my life as well. When the floor split fully open beneath me, I allowed my body to be swallowed up into it—disappearing into the hole to be presumed dead and gone. But instead, I fell through the space between and landed—rather than in the grave—upon the floor in the princess' nursery.

I had not lied when I said that I was a creature of honour, and though I felt broken, I had not come here to take the little princess with me. Rather, I had come to say farewell.

In a stealthy manner, I made my way to her bassinet. Leaning down over it, I looked at the infant who was once again awake. The sight of her was a painful arrow to my heart, and I audibly gasped for breath. The fingers that reached out to her this time trembled with emotion as I attempted to steady myself.

"Plans have changed, Princess. You won't be coming home tonight like we had planned."

I needed to go. I could hear the rush of footsteps down the passageway outside the room. They were coming to make certain I had not taken her anyway.

"But I won't be leaving you—not truly. When you look to the shadows, I will be there."

I had invested too much into this—into her—at this point and it was not something I could just walk away from. There was only so much I was willing to lose after nearly three years of focusing on little else. I leaned over the bassinet a little more so that I could press a kiss to her forehead. In the space where my lips touched her skin a warm, golden light shone.

"Sleep well, Princess," I whispered, her bright eyes upon my face.

I slipped away into the shadows just as the door to her room opened and there was a rush of bodies filling the space —armed soldiers, Moritz and his small blade, and a frantic Katrin rushing to pull the dainty form from her bed. Imelda's cry of distress split the air just as I disappeared into the space between.

True to my word, I had left—but I was not gone.

ACKNOWLEDGMENTS

Thank you, firstly, for picking this novella out of all the available stories out there, and giving both myself, and Rumpel, a chance. Through this story I wanted to highlight who the true villain was in this age-old tale—the man who locked a young woman up in a tower and forced her to spin gold for him. I also had a question I wanted to answer for myself. Why did Rumpelstiltskin ask for the future queen's firstborn child? I hope that you enjoyed the answers I discovered along the way.

This is not the last of Rumpelstiltskin, nor the last of that sweet baby girl, Princess Imelda. Look for their story to be furthered in the full-length novel, Threads of Silver!

A huge thank you must go out to my writing squad, Elle and Lou. The two of you have kept me writing these past ten years, and without your encouragement this story never would have been written. Thank you for convincing me I could do it, and that it would be worth it. Thank you for being the poke I needed to keep me going, and for always being the loudest cheerleaders in my corner. Lou, thank you for my beautiful cover. You've helped give Spun Gold its face!

Pam, thank you for your edits of the original draft and for being another voice of encouragement telling me that I had the ability to do this.

Melana, you have always been, and will always be, one of my greatest champions. You had faith in my writing even when I didn't, and were one of those pushing me to keep at it. Always looking for my next story and showing interest in what I was working on. Thank you for never letting me forget my first love—writing. You were never afraid of my imagination, but instead were the one who helped it grow. Where would I be without our childhood of make believe?

Thank you to my parents. Mom, you fostered my love of reading by showing me your own love of it, and then my love of writing by always wanting to read what I had written. Dad, you will never know how much buying me that word processor meant to me when I was 12 years old. It was like magic at my fingertips. I love you both xoxo.

Rodney, thank you for letting me read to you my first 'novel' when we were little. I'm sure it was a terrible horror story, but you had the grace to be invested in my characters, and terribly upset when Brooklyn was thrown over that bridge. It's memories like that which have kept me writing all these years.

ABOUT THE AUTHOR

Christis Christie was born and raised in a small town in New Brunswick, Canada where she spent most of her time either reading someone else's book, or dreaming of writing her own. Her favourite thing to dive into is an epic fantasy, or anything else magical and wondrous that really allows her imagination to take her away.

She now lives on the East Coast in Halifax, Nova Scotia where she works as an event designer, putting her interior decorating degree to wonderful use. Whenever she's not busy magically transforming venues for her clients, Christis is working on her own writing.

Her other dreams consist of one day visiting Ireland so she can frolic over the hills, and owning a teacup Pomeranian she can cart around everywhere with her.

Here's a sneak peek of Christis' upcoming novel, Threads of Silver.

THREADS OF SILVER

CHRISTIS CHRISTIE

Midnight Tide

PUBLISHING

There once was a young princess with hair of the softest gold, and eyes of the brightest blue, who kept a secret companion in the darkness of the shadows. She was never alone, as this friend would come to her early in the morning, or late at night, when the rest of the castle lay fast asleep. This friend was there to sing her ancient lullabies when the world became too frightening, or simply hold her hand through the twisting, coiling confusion of the garden maze.

He taught her words of old as they wiled away the afternoons by the fountains, and buried palace treasures in the vineyard. He was there whenever she desired, and all she need do was call out his name. But it was a name that was not to be shared with anyone else. A precious name to be kept secret, lest some other little boy, or girl, would whisper it to the winds and whisk him away.

So, the princess told no one of her companion from the dark. Not her beautiful, loving mother, nor any of her four younger sisters. Even though there were moments of temptation—when the weight became almost too much for the young girl to bear, and the thought tickled at the back of her mind to share her secret with at least the baby. She had vowed never to speak of it to another soul, and princesses always remained true to their word.

Those in the castle who saw her walking and talking with her shadow friend spoke often of the young princess' peculiar habits and imaginations. Her secret companion was very happy to be thought of as nothing more than a figment of her young imagination and so encouraged this understanding throughout the royal home.

As the years passed, her companion became more than just a friend—a confidant, a teacher, and a source of consolation.

The princess lived in a kingdom of prosperity and health, one in which the people were happy, and their bellies full. They praised the king who kept their borders safe and the coffers filled with gold. The castle however, though painted in the bright colours of the sun and carved outside with statues of gleeful maenads, was oftentimes dark within.

The king, though mighty in the eyes of his people, and those of the world, was not a happy or pleasant man. He possessed all the things he could ever need without having the one thing that he truly wanted—a prince.

The lovely queen had born him five children over the years of their marriage, but alas, each one had come healthy and squalling into the world a girl. Five beautiful princesses did King Ernst have, but no prince to carry on his name. The lovely little girls—though a pleasing sight for all to behold—were a disappointment to him, and his dissatisfaction tainted the very sunshine that lighted upon their pretty heads.

Their mother, Queen Katrin, strove to make their days as happy as she was able, matching their father's indifference with every ounce of love she could muster. There were times when the little princess—first born of them all—wished to tell her mother of the secret friend that visited her from the shadows. Of anyone, her sweet mother would understand. Queen Katrin knew of magic herself and was renowned for having won the king's heart by spinning three rooms of straw into gold. A love story that was sung about in taverns by drunken knights to hopeful maidens; told by candlelight to sleepy girls tucked into bed, who dreamt of princes whose hearts could be won by any ordinary girl—if they but possessed a touch of magic.

However, not even her magically-touched mother could be told, no matter how often she wished to chase away the lingering sadness within her mother's eyes with a tale of wonder. It was a promise of silence to which he held her, and to which she remained true. Because the young princess, Imelda Leona Liese, Crown Princess of Germaine and heir to the throne, was a sweet, kind, and honourable girl.

She was perhaps nine years old the day her sister Ingrid began to ask about her shadow friend. The young Princess Imelda—known as Imelle by those dear to her—sat alone on a bench in the gardens, twisting a piece of grass about her finger. The morning had been long with tutors and lessons: how to be a lady; how to walk with grace; how to sit properly in a chair; how not to chew with one's mouth full and by all heaven and earth do not speak at this time. None of the things Imelle learned were actually things she wanted to know. She may have seemed young to most, but she was smart enough to see the way her father acted compared with how her mother acted and read the differences.

While the queen needed to be a lady, an example of refined perfection, the king was able to be loud and coarse, and do as he pleased for the sake of the kingdom. One day that would be Imelle's place, or at least that was what she had been told.

"I want to learn how to be a fierce king, like my father,"

Imelle spoke, eyes fixed on the grass wound about her finger rather than the slight figure to her right.

"You cannot be a king like your father," her companion argued, his small form seated upon a little stone fountain that trickled water merrily.

"And why ever not?" The princess spoke with indignation at this insult to her character.

"A princess cannot be a king; she must be a queen." Today he was dressed in a red suit jacket with gold thread work emblazoned along the lapels.

He looked far too regal for a casual day in the sun, thought Imelle, but then, he always did. It seemed, to Imelle, that her friend was always attempting to over-compensate for his actual appearance. Rumpel was a creature of slight stature, and to the common eye, would not be considered beautiful—his features too pointed, teeth a little sharp, skin that took on a sickly cast even in pure sunlight, and elongated elven ears that were an over-exaggeration of what should have been a lovely thing. However, Imelle looked upon Rumpel with fondness. The young princess didn't see the unpleasant sight that others might; instead, she saw her lifelong friend whom she loved.

"Well...why not? No one listens to the queen, and if I am to rule, I must be listened to." She was only speaking reasonably, she was sure of it—Rumpel did not agree.

"Princesses simply do not become kings; you will be Queen Imelda when you take the throne."

Actions heavy-laden with disgust, Imelle huffed in disagreement, and cast her blade of grass aside. He was nonplussed as her blue eyes glared at him from the corner of their lidded enclosure.

"Well, I believe that is a silly rule that ought to be changed. How else will I make them work?"

"You will have to make them listen to you, Imelle, you have the ability to do so."

"But Rumpel—"

"No." There was a finality to his tone as he spoke. "Do not continue those words with me. You are the Princess Imelda, and the world will fall to their knees at your command. You need only have the strength to see it so." He spoke with such surety it was almost as if he had seen it, or at the very least, hoped to speak it into truth.

"Strength." Imelle had often times been told she was stubborn, but was she strong? "Am I strong?"

Dark, unfathomable green eyes peered across the grass and into her own.

"Yes, Princess, you are strong."

Rumpel spoke with such conviction that it made it all the easier to believe. Perhaps she could be strong enough to command men as a queen—forget being a king.

"Melly, who are you speaking to?"

The voice was soft and confused, coming from just over her shoulder. Imelle turned slowly so that she could face her younger sister. Ingrid was but six years old and had—though they were trying to break her of it—a terrible habit of sucking her thumb. The offending digit was presently at the side of her tiny rosebud-lips, awaiting its return between them.

"No one, Dovey." Imelle fought the great urge to quickly look over at her companion, though she knew of his 'overlooking' spell which made him invisible to all humans, excluding Imelle.

Imelle was special, and his spell of overlooking had never worked on her. Even from a very young age, she had been able to see right through it.

"But I heard you. Who's Rumpel?" They were innocent

words, spoken by an innocent child. Yet they were dangerous words all the same.

Inside her chest, Imelle could feel the beating of her heart—pounding and tripping at an alarming rate.

"Rumpled," Imelle interjected quickly. "You misheard. I said that my skirt was looking rumpled."

Going back into the castle would mean that her shadow conversation for the day was at an end, but Ingrid must be sufficiently distracted to ensure she forgot what she had heard. Standing from her spot on the bench, Imelle granted her friend a quick glance and nod of farewell, and then stepped towards her sister.

"Do you see?" she asked, grasping a handful of delicate, satin skirt to pull out on display.

Ingrid examined it with great seriousness before nodding her heard. "It is terribly rumply, Melly, don't let Frau Hilda see it."

Frau Hilda was their governess, and a stickler for proper etiquette and well-dressed little princesses.

"I will do my best." Imelle took the hand of her sister—the one favoured by her mouth—and began to lead her back towards the castle.

"Why do you talk to yourself, Melly? Frau Hilda says that you are odd."

Imelle sighed and gave Ingrid's small hand a slight squeeze.

"Sometimes, there just isn't anyone else to listen."

The fact of the matter was, Rumpel had always been there, for longer than she could even remember. Not telling him her thoughts would feel strange and unnatural. However, speaking to a friend of her imagination was no longer as cute at nine as it had been at four, or even six.

Rumpel was her friend, her guardian, and he wasn't meant to be shared. It was a secret she had kept for all of her life. Today had been a close call, though, and it made her fear what the future might hold. Soon there would be more tutors, which meant more eyes of judgement upon her, and it would become increasingly more difficult to hide him.

With Ingrid's small hand clasped inside her own, Imelle led the two of them back towards the marble patio that would take them inside and return the young princess to where she was supposed to be.

"How did you escape Fraulein Jana's care?"

"We were playing hide and seek, I've won," Ingrid announced.

Within the depths of Ingrid's big, brown eyes was a gleam of smug satisfaction that left Imelle in no doubt that Fraulein Jana had not agreed to playing the game out of doors.

"Did Fraulein Jana say that you could hide outside in the garden?"

"She didn't say that I couldn't." Ingrid was striving for a look of innocence that did not convince her eldest sister.

"And I am sure that my little Dovey did not ask either. Did she?" Imelle tapped on the end of her sister's small, button nose, which resulted in a giggle of delight.

The giggle was interrupted by an exclamation of Ingrid's name as a terribly harried-looking Jana came down the steps onto the walkway in a flourish of blue skirts.

"Oh Princess! I am so glad that you found your sister. Please forgive me, we were playing, and she was meant to stay within the conservatory." Fraulein Jana was young compared to the rest of the adults who cared for them.

Once Frau Hilda's lessons on etiquette and reform had ended for the day, each girl was passed on to her respective handmaiden. Fraulein Jana had the misfortune of being responsible for the mischievous Princess Ingrid who often-times had been mistaken for an imp.

"Don't fear, Fraulein, my sister is safe and fully aware of

the very naughty way in which she behaved. Aren't you, Ingrid?" Imelle cast her sister a side eye.

"But she never said—" Ingrid began to protest, only to be cut short by her eldest sister.

"Or perhaps we should let Frau Hilda know she's been running off without permission."

Imelle caught the pinched look on Jana's face—the young handmaiden had no desire to suffer through the angry tongue lashings of the upset Hilda should it be known that her charge had wandered off unsupervised—and offered her a subtle shake of her head to reassure her she had no intentions of actually informing the pious governess. Scaring Ingrid into better behaviour was her intent.

"No!" Ingrid exclaimed. Just as Imelle had thought, the fear of Frau Hilda's punishment far outweighed the pleasure her mischief had given her. "I am very sorry, Fraulein Jana, and I promise not to do it again."

Imelle smiled a little as Jana stepped forward to take Ingrid's hand.

"Well, all is forgiven, little princess, but let's get you back inside out of the sun," Jana murmured to her soothingly as she led her off.

Jana glanced back to Imelle and mouthed a silent thank you, then the two climbed the smooth steps of the palace and stepped through its towering glass doors.

It seemed it was the duty of the eldest princess to always be dousing the fiery flames of panic of the others around her. Perhaps she truly would be able to make the armies of men listen to her without the title of King...

This time, it was Imelle who cast a look behind her in search of Rumpel, but her small confidante had disappeared, even to her eyes.

No matter how hard the little princess tried to keep the secret to herself, moments would arise where the falsehoods she had created to mask the truth of her friendship came under scrutiny. That day in the garden with Ingrid was not the only narrowly escaped exposure of Rumpel. As the years passed, there were many other moments when the truth of what lay hidden in the shadows of Hammondburg Palace was nearly revealed. Sometimes by mere chance, other times due to the persistence of her sisters, or the servants.

As she aged, it was no longer feasible to claim attachment to an imaginary friend, and instead, Imelda learned to hide her times with Rumpel—to speak only when they were alone, to choose secluded areas for their discussions, or at the very least, bring a book with her to make it seem as if she were reading aloud to herself. It was not ideal for two such close confidants, but working together made it possible.

Her moments spent with Rumpel were not the only thing to change. After her twelfth year had come upon her, Imelle was pleased to learn that she would be granted more in-depth teaching sessions than what Frau Hilda had to offer. Now there were intense tutors come from all over the kingdom to teach King Ernst's Heir Apparent all about philosophy, science, economics and the strategies of war.

These lessons were far more difficult, and her tutors far more exacting than Frau Hilda had ever been. They demanded an excellence from Imelle that up until that point, she hadn't realized she was capable of. Yet, there was a pride and satisfaction in accomplishing the tasks set out for her. Each new acquisition of knowledge felt strangely like conquering her own civilization. Each new well done, delivered by a pleased tutor, was one step closer to being the queen she needed to be—so she worked diligently. If ever there was a time when Imelle thought she saw pride in her father's eyes over something that she had done, it was during that time. Imelle's cleverness and mind for strategy were almost enough to make Ernst overlook the fact that she was not a male.

Being offered what was nearly her father's pride and approval was a heady sensation for the young princess— having grown up so used to scorn or complete indifference. The thought of it, however, and the need for more, gave Imelle courage to press on harder in her studies. Her dedication did not go unnoticed by any, but most genuinely, it was Rumpel who beamed with pride.

Though kept busy with her work, Imelle was often left alone in one part of the large palace library or another for durations of the day, which created opportunity for her shadow companion to join her. She did her best to handle the lessons on her own, but at times Rumpel's insights were too valuable to overlook. They made for a wonderful team— as had always been the truth—and Imelle loved being able to share the work with him and see the way he viewed each new scenario given to her.

What the princess had come to understand of her friend, was that he had travelled the world over and seen so very much. Because of this, there was a deep well of information within Rumpel that she always wished to access. One day, when she was queen and no longer had to cower in the shadows with their friendship, she would announce his existence to the world and declare him her advisor.

"What was it like to be alive during this battle?" Imelle asked late one afternoon, a large book open before her. In her hand was a lovely brown-feathered quill, a piece of parchment beneath her hand for the notations she was making, and a small well of ink set just out of reach of spilling, but not too far as to be a nuisance.

Rumpel released a startled chuckle at this question, and it caused Imelle to lift her eyes from the page to take in his features.

"How old do you believe me to be?" he asked from his position in a chair on the opposite side of the table.

Imelle studied him, a small frown developing between her brows as she contemplated this question. She had never put much thought into his age before this moment. Rumpel had always just seemed to be—as if there had never been a moment when he wasn't. While his face did not exactly speak of a long life lived throughout the ages, neither did it speak of youthfulness.

"I don't...know?" There was doubt in her voice as she offered this response.

"I was not alive for that battle," he informed her without ceremony, a dry look upon his face.

Imelle felt her cheeks flush slightly with the heat of embarrassment, and she ducked her head as a laugh escaped her. He hadn't been alive to see a battle take place three hundred years before, but that still did not answer the question of how old he actually was. Once more, her eyes left the history book before her so that she could study Rumpel.

"How old are you?"

"I am sixty-seven years," he responded dryly.

"Truly?" she asked, surprised. "But that...is old."

Once again, a dark chuckle slipped from Rumpel's lips at her words, and he shook his head at her ever so slightly before responding. "In the elven world, I am not yet considered to be of adult years."

Imelle knew there was shock registering upon her face as he spoke these words, for it felt as if her world had spun a little on its axis, setting everything off-kilter just a fraction. Rumpel had always felt very much like a guardian of sorts to her. In many ways, he was the father Ernst refused to be. So, to learn that in the mind of his people he was not much older than herself was shocking.

"Truly?"

"Truly."

"Does this mean..." Imelle wasn't even quite certain how to ask what she was presently feeling.

"Things have to change?" As usual, he already knew exactly what she was thinking, so that words were not necessary. "No, my princess, we are as we have always been, and as we will always be. Age is but a number, and no matter what others may think of me, I will always be your godfather."

Imelle felt a wave of relief rush over her and wash away the fragments of fear splintering in her mind. She did not want to lose the one thing she had always been able to count on.

"You are more than a godfather, Rumpel, you are my best friend."

He smiled warmly at her, putting the subtle points of his teeth on display, and while it could have appeared sinister, to Imelle it was endearing.

"Thank you. Now, stop finding distractions all around you and focus on that battle which I was most certainly not alive to witness."

Laughter spilled out of Imelle as she ducked her head back down to her book, a smile catching at her lips and remaining there as she returned to the work at hand. The history of the battle, which was detailed in all its gruesome glory, was a difficult read, and yet she found it fascinating. Soon enough her mind was caught back up in her study, the quill scratching over parchment with quick, confident strokes as she wrote important facts she would need to report back to her tutor later.

As she made her notations, Imelle's mind drifted to the truth of Rumpel's age and what she had assumed simply because she had never thought to seek clarification. All that had been required was the right question, and there had been ample opportunity throughout their friendship for her to ask it. Her mind continued to work. How many problems arose in their kingdom because her father was too stubborn to ask the right questions? King Ernst was not the sort of man Imelle could imagine finding the patience to get to the true heart of a problem, not when it was between people of lesser means who had no real connection to him.

Perhaps she was wrong, but she had born witness to the anger within the king firsthand.

The misfortune had only befallen her once, but it was not a sight anyone was likely to forget, least of all a young girl of seven. It was the day of sweet Anja's birth, while the church bells tolled to announce the royal birth, King Ernst railed in fury that his wife had born him yet another daughter. A fury that only increased in tempo and heat after the midwife conferred with the royal chirurgeon and notified him that the queen had nearly lost her life bringing the infant into the world, and should she try for another, it would likely take her and the child from the world.

Imelle had snuck out of her room with the notion that she would go into her mother's chambers and see her new little sister for the first time—she wasn't meant to be out in the hallway at all—but the way in was blocked by her father throwing what, by most, would be called a tantrum. However, it was a tantrum of terrifying proportions which quickly had the eldest princess hiding behind a woven tapestry on the wall.

Crouching there in the darkness of the fabric, Imelle had watched as her father took hold of a suit of armour decorating the hallway and tossed it to the floor in an ear-deafening crash of metal and chain mail colliding with carved stone. It made the little girl tremble in fear and uncertainty as she shrank further into her hiding place.

There, in the darkness of the tapestry, Imelle had listened to her father roar at the failure of her mother and watched as he ripped paintings from the wall. It was the first time the young princess had ever really been made aware of the anger that could reside within an adult, most specifically her father. It made her fear for her mother's safety and for that of her newborn sister. In the end, he had calmed himself enough that he was able to go in and see both mother and child, but not until dawn's rays had begun to grace the earth outside.

Having seen that man, witnessed the darkness of his displeasure, Imelle wasn't certain he had the patience as king to listen to the woes of the common man, or to deal with petty conflict. She wanted to be different, to know of having a firm hand when righting wrongs and an ear that was open to the plight of the weak and needy. Was there a way to have the terrifying fierceness of her father but also the tenderness of her mother? Could those things co-exist in the same person, and if so, how was it she went about obtaining those qualities?

As the years continued to drift slowly by, bringing more age and experience to the young princess, that question remained in the forefront of her mind. Was she becoming the strong, independent woman who would fiercely command armies with but the lift of a finger, and in the next breath welcome her people to her bosom in tenderness and understanding? Would her father allow for that kind of softness within her?

The shadow of pride he had shown at her determination and dedication in her studies had not lasted long, and soon he was complaining that there was too much softness in her voice when she spoke. Complaining that she didn't show enough spine when dealing with conflict. Which wasn't true, it was simply that when faced with her father, Imelle soon found herself backing down—her inner seven-year-old emerged and she was returned to that night behind the tapestry. Once he had worked himself into one of these particular rants where it concerned her, it wouldn't take long before Imelle was hearing about how things would be different if she had been born a boy. That she wouldn't be so tender, or so lenient, if she were a man.

His lack of a male heir would never be an ill he was finished lamenting.

During the times when she began to doubt her ability to be the queen that was needed, Rumpel did whatever he could to encourage her, and when Rumpel wasn't available, there was her mother.

Queen Katrin had a steady quality about her that had kept her shoulders straight and her chin up no matter the torrent of disapproval that had come her way throughout the years of her marriage. To Imelle, her mother was the perfect example of how to be tender, yet strong. By many it was considered the queen's one true job, to produce heirs, and if she failed to do so then she failed in the only duty she was intended for. Queen Katrin had produced five heirs, but none of them the gender her husband had so vehemently desired.

Still she stood steadfast at his side each evening as they welcomed the guests of the castle to the evening meal and sat primly in the smaller throne beside his own as they met delegates sent by other countries or heard the testimony of battling lords. Not once did she falter, never did unhappiness or despair show upon her features and, there was always a smile of greeting curving her lips when required. Lady Katrin, Queen of Germaine was a core of wrought iron covered in a delicate sheath of elegance and grace.

Imelle was fifteen when she found the nerve one evening to ask her mother if she had been mistaken in marrying the king. It was a rare evening when just the two of them were able to spend some time together, the other girls having gone to their own chambers and the king having left on a hunting trip in the southern province.

"Mother, do you ever regret becoming queen?" she asked from her place on the floor, a soft rug of bear's skin beneath her and a flickering fire casting a warm glow and comforting heat from the hearth.

Imelle had joined her mother in her chambers where she was busy working on a quilted piece to be hung on the wall. It was a glorious hanging, each small piece of colourful fabric stitched on perfectly to depict a scene of great bravado— King Ernst spearing a wild boar on foot, his horse rearing in fright in the background. It was the hunting story her father was known for sharing at large banquets when he sought to impress delegations from another country with his prowess and bravery in the face of danger.

Her mother's work was beautiful, each stitch perfect and

the detail of the scene almost too much to believe. Imelle felt a little frightened merely touching the hanging, knowing that her own stitching was not nearly as elegant or practiced as her mother's, but it was about the time spent together rather than what she could offer to the work. Which was also why as she sat there on the floor with her legs folded beneath her, it was a side seam she was finishing up rather than the detailed quilting work her mother was doing in the center.

"No, I do not," was the steady response from her mother, who hadn't even bothered to look up from her work.

However, Imelle did, glancing up to where her mother sat in a high-backed wing chair, the wall hanging draped over her lap as she stitched around the colourful figures to make them stand out.

"Never?" Imelle couldn't help the doubt filling her at her mother's response. "Not even the night Anja was born?"

This time, her mother's head lifted and Imelle found herself pierced with a disconcerting look. The queen had not been aware of Imelle's presence that night—no one had been.

"What do you know of that night?" Her mother was remaining calm, but Imelle was able to see the subtle lines that had developed at the corner of her eyes. It was a sure sign she was concerned over the news being shared with her.

"I was outside in the hall when Father learned you could have no more children. I've never seen him so angry as he was that night... I know he did not go to see you, or Anja, until the next morning." Her own lips were pursing together in a strong line of disapproval. Her mother had nearly died and still, her father couldn't be bothered to go in and check on them.

"Oh Imelda...you should not have seen that." Her mother spoke with tenderness, overlooking the question that had been asked in preference of consoling her for something that had happened many years earlier.

"Preferably not, but I did." Imelle's eyes met those of her mother's, mirrored pools of the same colour reflecting back at each other. "But did you not regret it, even for a moment, once that night had passed? You almost *died*, and he just...ignored that fact." There was a sliver of contempt in her tone as she spoke, her mind drifting back to that night. It was not an outrageous assumption to think anyone would regret their choices following that period.

This time her mother's response was not so quick to come, which made it seem more believable once she finally spoke.

"No, Imelda, even then I did not regret my decision."

"But how?" Did her mother not realize she deserved better than that?

"Because I made the choice to marry your father knowing full well what sort of man he was."

"You...did?" But why would anyone?

"I did. There were expectations of me, and unpleasant outcomes if I were to turn down his offer, but I did it knowing what sort of life awaited me." Her mother sighed, seeing the disbelief written clearly upon her daughter's face. "And I can tell exactly what you are thinking."

Imelle huffed and turned to look at the fire, doubting very much that her mother knew *exactly* what she was thinking.

"Sometimes we are faced with difficult decisions that might not be precisely what we had dreamed for our lives, or the ideal situation for our complete happiness, but they are the best choice moving forward. The most important thing about any decisions that we make, hard or easy, is that we make them with our eyes open. Imelle..." She was saying her name with the implication that she wanted her daughter to look at her.

Sighing, Imelle turned her head to comply, their eyes

meeting once more over the beautiful spread of embroidery and quilting.

"Your life will be filled with hard decisions, and often-times they will be ones you do not want to make, but know that you must. These decisions won't always be easy, nor make you happy, but they won't always be terrible decisions either. You might question why I chose to marry your father knowing the darkness that lay inside him, but what you forget is that from this marriage I have received great joy, as well."

Imelle allowed her eyes to drift over her mother's face, noting how the stress lines had smoothed around her eyes and her previous relaxed appearance had returned.

"You and your sisters are my pride and joy—no matter what any of your father's advisors may say. I am not sorry you failed to be born male, and I believe wholeheartedly that you will make a remarkable ruler once your time comes. My decision to marry your father and become queen led to you. So no, I do not, for even one moment, regret that choice."

Imelle could feel a soft flush of happiness warming her cheeks and she ducked her head in a bashful manner, attempting to look like she was concentrating on her needle-work rather than trying to hide her face. She had never doubted her mother's love for a moment, but it was still a wonderful thing to hear the words.

"Thank you, Mama."

Queen Katrin did her best to instil in all of them the knowledge that life was not always easy, even for those of the nobility, and that they must be prepared for hard choices. That hard choices were a part of the expectations of their lives. Eventually each girl would be required to marry, and not for love, but for the betterment of the kingdom. They would not lead armies into battle, but they could wed husbands who would bring with them great armies to support the Kingdom of Germaine in all of her endeavours.

However, with these lessons, was also their mother's hope that they would not dwell upon the negative, and instead find for themselves whatever happiness they could in their impending situations.

Imelle didn't like this way of thinking. Why, just because they had been born female, did they have to settle for whatever was handed to them? Knowing full well what marriage to the wrong sort of person could bring into one's life, she had no desire to see that fate foisted upon herself or any of her younger sisters.

As she grew, the young princess settled within herself that she would do whatever it took to give herself, and her sisters, the chance for true happiness. Between herself and Rumpel there must be something that could be done to change the course of five princesses headed towards marriages of political gain and intrigue.

Her mother might believe that some decisions were inevitable, but Imelda, future Queen of Germaine, had to believe that fates could be rewritten, and old ways remade.

CHAPTER THREE

*A*ge Seventeen

"Imelda Leona Liese! Do not tell me that you've explicitly ignored what was asked of you this morning. That you were romping down alleyways like some poor, motherless street urchin!"

Imelle winced at the scolding tone making its way to her from beyond the printed screen concealing her from view. She hurriedly bound the servant's garments up into a tight ball to be shoved behind the stand bearing her washing basin and mirror. If Frau Hilda found the dress, bonnet, and apron, they would be taken away and likely burned out of rage for her continual, defiant behaviour. Acquiring the garments in the first place had taken some maneuvering on her part, and Imelle had no desire to try her hand at it once more.

"Would you prefer I say no....or give you the truth?" Imelle called out, grinning a little at her own cheeky response as she reached for the bar of soap. Dousing it in the water basin, she began scrubbing at her fingertips, knowing that Hilda would be incensed should she see the filth presently beneath her nails.

It wasn't that she was always running rampant in the streets and digging through dirt as any common man, but today she and Rumpel had run into a little more trouble than their typical excursions incited. After a tumble out a window into a garbage heap, the princess had returned looking rather worse for wear, causing her handmaiden to gasp in horror, and flee in search of Frau Hilda. Traitorous fiend.

There was a long-suffering sigh from beyond the screen and Imelle knew she was driving the poor old woman to near distraction with her antics, but it wasn't something she seemed capable of ceasing—or at least wasn't willing to. The princess appreciated the ability to go down into the city proper and experience the lives of the people there. It was her desire to understand them, their needs, and their problems, just a little better. Most commonly, Rumpel would cast his spell of overlooking on both of them so that her presence went entirely unnoticed.

Imelle wasn't foolish, she knew that the heir to the throne heading down into the city unescorted by guards could be a dangerous thing, which was why she did her best to remain hidden. However, there were times when it felt imperative that she interact with the citizens one on one, and it was for these moments that she wore the servant's garments. Up until today, their ruse had succeeded in its intent—keeping her safe, and concealed.

All good things must come to an end, however, and while she was visiting with the elderly mother of a cobbler, one of her father's advisors had entered the small shop to have the soles of his boots repaired. Rumpel had quickly pointed to the window behind the elderly woman as a means of escape. It wasn't much of a drop, but what lay below was unpleasant —old boots and shoes, scraps of hide, and other forms of unmentionable items. However, fearing discovery, and knowing that the outcome of being found there would be far worse than whatever awaited her in the pile, she had pushed herself out the window and landed in a heap of skirts amongst the rubbish.

Clawing herself out of the heap had been more than unpleasant, but once she was free from it, Rumpel's spell was upon them again and they both headed back towards the palace. The narrow escape had left Imelle feeling exuberant and full of life. The sensation had lasted right up until the point Ulla had stared at her in horror and then rushed off to inform Frau Hilda of what she had been doing.

Frau Hilda, who was presently grumbling under her breath as she worked her way around Imelle's room, organizing items for the night's feast.

"It's okay, I've come back in one piece." Imelle stuck her head out from behind the screen to offer the governess a reassuring smile, but was met with a storm cloud of disapproval.

Honestly, she was too old for a governess, but no one else was deemed stern enough to shepherd the eldest princess into appropriate behaviour on a daily basis. Many had tried without success until the task had been appointed to the girls' matronly governess—a woman of indomitable fortitude and a strict sense of etiquette and moral high ground.

"No, Princess, it is far from okay. You were given specific instructions this morning on how you were to spend your day, at which time you gave me your word. Your word that has now been broken. If a princess' word means nothing, then what does she stand for?"

The cheeky, self-satisfied grin that had set upon her face soon lost its perch, unseated by Hilda's poignant scolding that promptly hit its intended mark. There were a lot of things in this world that a person could not count on, but Imelle did not want her word to be lumped in with that lot. If she could not be trusted, what worth did she hold?

Reaching for the soft towel set beside the water basin, Imelle slowly dried her hands as she came from behind the screen, a remorseful air to her appearance.

"You are correct, Frau Hilda, and I apologize. Not because I left the palace when I was not supposed to, but because I promised you first that I wouldn't." An apology was only good if it were honest and true, so she would not apologize for something she did not mean, but offered Hilda the truth.

Her governess nodded her aged head, the wiry wisps of her hair peeking out from beneath her cotton bonnet.

"Come, into the tub with you. I refuse to send Her Royal Highness down to her own name day celebration covered in street grime."

Without further ado, Imelle pulled the white cotton chemise up over her head, and allowed it to drop to the floor, followed soon by her pantaloons as she crossed over to the copper tub currently steaming in the middle of her room. Carefully climbing into it, she sank down into the hot water with a slight hiss, and then settled with her knees drawn up and arms looped loosely around them. Old fingers, still deft at their task, unpinned the crown of hair about her head until it lay loose around her shoulders. Closing her eyes, Imelle held her breath as the first pitcher of water came cascading down over her face.

It was a sign of Hilda's irritation with her actions today that she was handling the task of bathing her instead of leaving it to her handmaidens. Clearly, Imelle was not to be trusted on her own until she was well and truly situated in the banqueting hall.

"Whatever do you get yourself up to in the city? It is no place for a young woman of your status and importance, Princess," Hilda scolded, dousing her head with another pitcher of water before she began to work soap into her hair. The strong scent of it making Imelle's nose scrunch.

"I've told you...I simply want to understand how the common people live."

A lightly mocking chuckle greeted these words.

"Why are you laughing?" Imelle questioned, her back stiffening with offence.

"You won't find the common folk in Potsdamburg. The truly needy lie outside the city walls, out in the countryside where His Grace's riches rarely reach."

Imelle felt a frown slipping over her features, and she turned her head a little so that she could gaze at Hilda kneeling by the side of the tub.

"Are there a great many? I thought the kingdom was prosperous."

"The prosperity of a kingdom often comes off the backs of the common citizen. He dedicates his life to working for that very prosperity, and while he may be compensated financially for his troubles, there is no cure for his crippled body nor a way to rewind the years lost toiling for someone else's gain."

Imelle knew enough from her trade and commerce lessons to question just how well the farmers were compensated for their efforts. Anything that came to the castle to be sent off for trade purposes would have prices exponentially raised so that the Royal Treasury profited. What kind of profit did the families responsible for all of the work actually see, though?

"I suppose I've never really thought about the distribution of that wealth," she admitted.

"Your heart is in the right place with your efforts, Princess, but the capital city is not the place to look for true poverty." With that said, Hilda pressed fingers to her jaw and gently pushed her face forward once more so that she could return to washing her hair.

As her head was jostled back and forth from Hilda's

vigorous scrubbing, Imelle allowed her mind to wander. What were the chances that her father would allow her to take a personal trip outside the city? She doubted very much it would be seen as something worth the time and efforts of the guards who would have to accompany her.

Once every inch of her skin had been scrubbed raw by the coarse cloth in Hilda's hand, and her form inspected for any forgotten spot or imperfection, Imelle was allowed to climb free of the tub and dry off. Soon she found herself dressed once more in stockings, pantaloons and a fresh chemise covering her heat-flushed skin.

Ulla was at last allowed to return to the room once Imelle was seated before her mirror and ready for her hair to be tended to. While it seemed Ulla could not be trusted to keep Imelle's indiscretions to herself, she was gentle with her brushing and did her best never to pull the hair more than was needed to remove the knots and tangles. Which was a kindness, as the torture of her corset was still to come. Carefully, the long strands of her golden hair were brushed until the silken strands shone like sunshine, and then Ulla began to braid and pin her hair up into an elaborate style fixed with jewelled pins.

"Are you excited for the celebrations tonight, Miss?" Ulla asked, fixing the last strand into place. She smiled at Imelle in the mirror.

"I suppose it will be fun, I know Greta is looking forward to the ball to follow." Imelle stood, and moved to slip into her corset, then gripped the bed post as Ulla began to tighten the ties.

"Princess Greta looks so very pretty when dancing," Ulla commented, giving a hard yank on her laces.

Imelle let out a harsh breath which filtered off into a wheeze as her ribs were constricted by boning.

"She does, and has practiced diligently for tonight. Ingrid is very upset she isn't old enough to attend."

"It's hard for younger sisters to watch while their older sisters are able to do things they are not," Ulla spoke, giving another harsh tug.

"It's also a necessary evil, and one that builds character," Hilda rasped from her place on the other side of the room where she was busy preparing Imelle's gown.

"I believe Ingrid would argue with that," Imelle stated, letting out another grunt as her entire body was jostled by Ulla's work.

Once it was nearly impossible to breathe, Ulla declared her ready for her dress, and moved over to Hilda's side to assist her in bringing the cream-coloured gown over. Bending over a little, Imelle allowed her head to be worked carefully through the layer upon layer of satin and tulle until it popped up through the open neckline. With Ulla's help, she slipped her arms through the short-capped sleeves and stood so that the remainder of the dress could be pulled into place.

The soft satin shimmered as she shifted, her hands smoothing the full skirt around her hips while Ulla pulled on the lacing in the back. The gown had a low, square neckline that skimmed just overtop her moderate bust, and all along its short sleeves was a mix of navy and turquoise embroidery, dotted with sparkling gems. Her corset helped to increase the effect of her slim waist, the bodice of the gown cinched narrowly above her hips and pointed down towards the full skirt that swished and rustled with the slightest movement.

The elaborate navy and turquoise embroidery formed branches of sparkling leaves all down the front of the skirt and circled around the entire bottom, creating a wide band that would gleam and twinkle with each step she took that night. It was a beautiful dress, one that had been commissioned specifically for her name day.

"You look lovely, Princess," Ulla praised, moving to grab her golden-threaded dancing slippers.

"Thank you, Ulla." Imelle smiled a little at her, reaching down to gather up handfuls of her heavy skirt so that she could step into the gold slippers her handmaid placed on the floor before her.

"Yes, she looks lovely. Now let's see if she can manage to behave the same."

Both Imelle and Ulla turned their heads to look at Hilda at the same time. However, while Ulla was nodding her head in agreement at such sage words, Imelle was scowling just a hair.

"Don't give me that look, Princess. This may be your name day celebration, but there are a great many influential people attending this evening, and it will not do to upset His Grace."

Hilda had a point, as she usually did, but it would have been appreciated if the older woman had at least offered Imelle the benefit of a doubt before automatically assuming she was going to wind up doing something to cause a commotion that night.

"I will be on my best behaviour tonight, you have my word. My *honest* word," she corrected herself, wanting Hilda to know that she could trust her to behave.

The last thing the princess wanted for herself was to end the night with her father upset at her. It was rare that he was exceedingly pleased, but with Ernst, his indifference could be just as desired.

With everything else about her in place and ready, the final item brought to adorn her was the golden tiara, crafted especially for her seventeenth year. An intricate work of branches bearing delicate golden leaves that gleamed in the faint candlelight flickering on her walls. Imelle stood still as Ulla nestled it upon her head, amongst the coiled braids and gems that were a result of Ulla's earlier handiwork.

The weight of the tiara upon her head was not unfamiliar, and now that her body was constricted and her head heavy, she felt like the courtly mask had settled upon her and she was ready to go downstairs.

"Am I ready? Is it time?"

Frau Hilda gave her one last look over as Ulla stepped to the side, and she nodded her head.

"Yes, you are ready. Happy name day, Princess."

Tales of the Sea Witch by Lou Wilham

No creature under the sea is born dark; some just lose themselves.

Irsa's name was lost long ago to the obscurity of being labeled a villain. Born with enough magic to boil the ocean, all Irsa wants is a simple life with her best friend, Aislin. But when they discover their connection is more than just friendship, the pair must fight all odds to be together.

Surviving the sea isn't easy, but Irsa has never known any different. With Aislin by her side, she must face a wicked witch, defy a prince, and maybe gain all she ever wanted: a happily ever after.

Add to your TBR
Purchase Today

Tin by Candice Robinson & Amber R. Duell

Tin is the most famous fae in Oz for all the wrong reasons. Cursed with a stone heart, he is the perfect assassin: ruthless, efficient, and merciless with thousands of kills to his name. When his old friend, Lion, offers him a small fortune to deliver Dorothy to the South for his lover to wear the girl's head as her own, Tin doesn't hesitate to accept the unsavory deal.

Dorothy Gale lost everything—her family to illness, her dog to age, and now her farm to foreclosure. The entire town thought she was crazy for believing in a faerie world called

Oz, but even after ten years have passed, she can't help knowing she was right. So when an emerald green portal opens in her wheat field, she jumps at the opportunity to return to the only place she ever felt like she belonged.

Tin wasn't expecting a grown woman to step through the portal, just as Dorothy wasn't expecting Tin to have his stone heart back, but Oz holds more unexpected things than either could have imagined. Magic has hidden dangerous lies behind glamour, trapped innocents in curses, and left the land of Oz in turmoil—none more so than the South. As Tin and Dorothy travel together for the second time in a decade, their lives begin to make sense again. Soon, they must decide who to give their loyalties to before Lion takes Dorothy's head and Tin's cursed heart is forever doomed.

Coming Soon
12.09.20

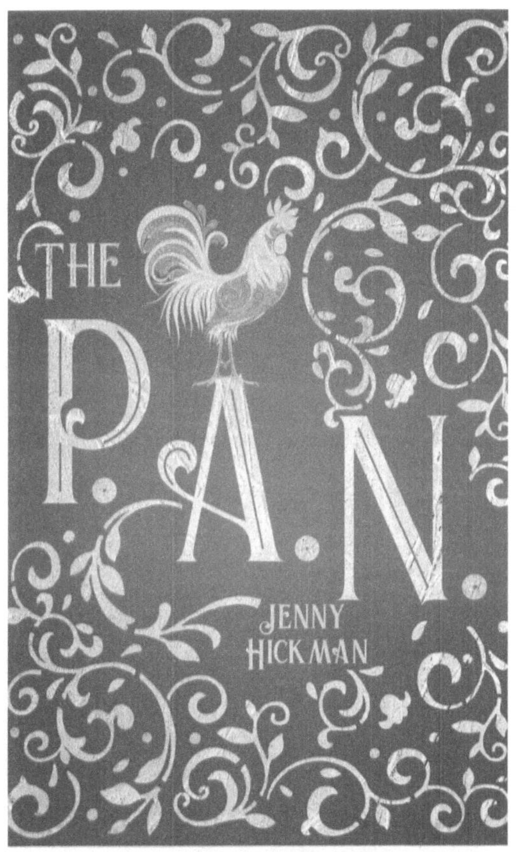

The P.A.N. by Jenny Hickman

Since her parents were killed, Vivienne has always felt ungrounded, shuffled through the foster care system. Just when liberation finally seems possible—days before her eighteenth birthday—Vivienne is hospitalized with symptoms no one can explain.

The doctors may be puzzled, but Deacon, her mysterious new friend, claims she has an active Nevergene. His far-fetched diagnosis comes with a warning: she is about to become an involuntary test subject for Humanitarian Organization for Order and Knowledge—or HOOK. Vivienne can either escape to Neverland's Kensington Academy and learn to fly (Did he really just say fly?) or risk sticking around to become a human lab rat. But accepting a place among The PAN means Vivienne must abandon her life and foster family to safeguard their secrets and hide in Neverland's shadows… forever.

Add to your TBR
Purchase Today